The Mall

He started away, paused for a second, then turned slightly, looking back at her over his shoulder. Trish busied herself with the baker's rack at the rear of the stand, and when she finally turned around again, he had gone.

Immensely relieved, she sagged back against the wall, putting one hand to her heart. There'd been something so unsettling about that man — something so weirdly different — and she suddenly realized she was shaking. She was sure he'd left The Eatery, yet she could still see him — the dark, blank circles where his eyes should have been, the unusual ash-gray color of his hair and beard.

Just a crazy, she argued to herself. *Just your usual eccentric customer.*

Nothing to get upset about...

Look out for:

Thirteen Again
Various

Nightmare Hall:
The Scream Team
Diane Hoh

The Forbidden Game 2:
The Chase
L.J. Smith

Point Horror

THE MALL

Richard Tankersley Cusick

■SCHOLASTIC

Scholastic Children's Books,
7-9 Pratt Street, London NW1 0AE, UK
a division of Scholastic Publications Ltd
London ~ New York ~ Toronto ~ Sydney ~ Auckland

First published in the US by Simon & Schuster Inc., 1992
First published in the UK by Scholastic Publications Ltd, 1995

Copyright © Richie Tankersley Cusick, 1992

ISBN 0 590 13158 3

Printed by Cox and Wyman Ltd, Reading, Berks

10 9 8 7 6 5 4 3 2 1

*To my editor, Pat MacDonald, whose wisdom
gives wings to my writing.*

Prologue

It was a game of his . . . standing in the store window . . . hiding among the mannequins as if he were lifeless, too, and one of them.

He was very good at it.

It was one of the things he had learned to do best.

All those hours of practice.

But what else did he have, really, but time.

Hours and days and weeks and months of sitting there in his room . . . in the cool, damp dark . . . and he could stare for hours and hours on end, not moving so much as a muscle—just staring . . . and thinking . . . just dreaming of her.

Her.

And now—at last—he had seen her tonight.

He was almost certain she worked here, in the mall.

He had seen her with two friends, and they had been laughing, and her brown hair was long and thick and soft, and her blue eyes were clear like summer skies, and her laugh was bright like sun.

He had imagined how she would feel—her skin . . . her lips . . . her wonderful hair. . . .

He had imagined how she would feel the whole time he stared at her, the whole time he was frozen with the mannequins in the store window, and her walking right past him, smiling up at him, but not knowing—not knowing he was there.

That he was watching her.

And afterward—afterward—he had run down to the safe, dank places, where he could think . . . where he could make his plans . . .

She's the one.

She's the one I want.

But not yet, he decided.

Not quite yet.

Not until everything was perfect.

1

Didn't I tell you you'd love working here?" Nita Hanson peered at her friend over the top of the counter and immediately pointed out two gigantic muffins in the glass display case. "I want those. And be sure to take out the calories."

Trish Somerfield smiled and reached for a paper bag. "You just want to make me fat. That's why you got me this job at The Eatery instead of at one of the shops—so I'd get too big for all my clothes."

"Right. And then you can give them all to me. Especially the red sweater with the dark blue trim." Nita tossed her head, her short blond hair falling back perfectly around her pretty face. "Anyway, I know a food court's not particularly glamorous, but this was the only job opening I knew about. And *anyway,* you wouldn't *want* to be working in *my* store today, I promise you."

"No?" Trish popped the muffins into the sack and

handed them to her friend, pausing a moment to ponder the register.

"I'm telling you, weird things happen at this mall," Nita shook her head. "Gives me the creeps."

"What weird things?"

"You can't tell anyone." Nita leaned closer and lowered her voice. "I'm not even supposed to be saying this, because they don't like rumors getting started around here. They're always afraid it'll scare off customers."

Trish nodded and handed Nita her change.

"Okay, I get to work this afternoon, right?" Nita opened the bag and pulled out one of the muffins, prying a walnut loose with one perfectly manicured fingernail. "So Pat—she's my manager—tells me she got a call this morning before the mall even opened— the store was unlocked—the doors weren't even closed."

"You're kidding." Trish frowned back at her. "Were you robbed?"

"No, that's just it. The money was still in the register. Freida—she was supposed to stay late and close last night—hadn't cleaned up or counted the drawer or anything."

"So what happened? Did she just leave?"

"No one knows. I was off yesterday, but the night before, she and Pat had this *huge* fight—so the first thing I think of is that she's trying to get back at Pat, right? But nobody can even *find* Freida to ask her what happened."

"What do you mean, they can't find her?"

"I mean, she's not at her house. I guess some neighbor said she was supposed to leave on a trip last night after work, but he doesn't know where she is or when she'll be back."

4

Trish glanced back over her shoulder and straightened up. "I have to go. *My* manager is giving me the evil eye."

"I've heard about her." Nita made a face. "What's her name again? And is she as mean as everyone says she is?"

"Her name's Bethany, and she *is* mean," Trish sighed. "She's been giving me a bad time ever since I started working here."

"How come?" Nita turned to stare, but Trish pushed her gently away.

"Don't get me in trouble. She must just have this thing about new employees or something. *I* can't figure it out."

"Maybe she thinks you're after her job."

"Right. My all-consuming, burning passion in life is to be the full-time manager of Muffin-Mania."

As they both broke into giggles, Nita grabbed Trish's arm and pointed toward Pizza Park several cubicles away.

"Look—he's here today—how can you stand the excitement?"

"Will you *stop?*" Trish forced Nita's hand from her sleeve and slammed it down on the counter. "Nothing like being obvious—"

"I *never* have trouble remembering *his* name," Nita sighed. "Storm Reynolds. With a name like that, he should be in the movies."

"With you as his leading lady, I suppose."

Nita kept staring. "He is *so* gorgeous."

"I know."

"And he's looking right at you."

"He is not."

"Yes, he is."

As Trish shook her head insistently, Nita gave her a

shove, forcing her to take a reluctant peek at the object of their conversation.

He was tall—well over six feet—and slender but well built, with broad shoulders and leanly muscled forearms. As he leaned forward to slide some trays of pizza into the ovens, his thick dark hair fell over his forehead, and a fine sheen of sweat shone across his high cheekbones. He straightened up, wiping one arm casually across his face, and as Trish continued to watch him, he suddenly glanced at her and winked, the corners of his mouth lifting in an amused smile.

"Oh, no, he saw me." Flustered, Trish turned back to Nita and gave *her* a shove. "Go on, get out of here. I can't believe this. I'm so embarrassed."

"And you said he wasn't looking," Nita chided gently. "Ask him out."

"I will not."

"Go ahead. I dare you."

"I don't take dares."

"You should take this one. It's too good to pass up."

"Get out of here."

"Well, all I'm trying to do is prove to you how cute you are. You never think guys are looking at you— and *I* notice guys looking at you all the time."

"Oh, Nita, will you *please*—"

"Like—like—" Nita reached out and pulled on Trish's sleeve. "Like *that* guy there."

"What guy where?"

"Over there. Reading the newspaper."

"Nita, how can that guy be looking at me and reading his paper at the same time?"

"Oh, okay, so he's not looking at you now. But a *second* ago he was looking at you. He was downright *staring* at you!"

"Nita," Trish gave a long, tolerant sigh, "listen to

6

me. I'm standing in a muffin booth. Right in the middle of the food court. Right in the middle of the mall. Every single person who walks through here looking for something to eat *has* to look at me sooner or later!"

"Well, he *was* looking at you," Nita said stubbornly.

"Was he drooling?" Trish tried to keep a straight face.

"Probably."

"Were his eyes longing with desire?"

"I don't know. He had sunglasses on."

"Well, that makes a lot of sense, Nita. And that's definitely the kind of guy I've always dreamed about. One who sits inside and reads his paper with sunglasses on."

"Okay, go ahead and make fun. But when he turns out to be some famous celebrity who doesn't want to be mobbed, and he goes back to his billion-dollar mansion all alone 'cause you *snubbed* him, don't blame me."

"I promise I won't." Trish glanced around surreptitiously and sneaked another muffin into Nita's bag. "Flattery will get you everywhere. Now go back to work."

"You'll be sorry," Nita shook her head in mock sympathy, folding down the top of her bag, backing away from the counter. "When you find out I'm right, you'll just be the sorriest girl in the world 'cause you snubbed that guy behind the paper."

"And you'll be sorry if you get fired!"

"Come get me for dinner! I can go anytime."

"Okay—see you later."

As Nita walked off, Trish busied herself wiping off the counter, only stopping to look up again when she felt someone tap her firmly on the arm.

"You're here to work, not to socialize," Bethany said crisply. "I suggest you concentrate on your job and not on your friends."

"I—" Trish gulped, wiping her hands nervously on her apron. "I'm sorry—I wasn't exactly busy—I didn't think—"

"Well, next time *do* think," Bethany said coldly. "If you were conscientious, you'd notice that there are *always* things that need to be done around here. Nobody has time in my area to just stand around and goof off."

Without waiting for Trish to answer, she stalked away, leaving the startled girl to stare after her, openmouthed.

"Wow," Trish mumbled to herself, picking up her rag again, giving the countertop another swipe. "I guess *she* told *me.*"

"One honey muffin, please."

Startled, Trish saw a hand slide toward her across the counter, and she instinctively drew back as the long tapered fingers unfolded, revealing a crumpled five-dollar bill inside. For a minute she thought it was a woman who had spoken, yet as she lifted her eyes from the pale, smooth palm, she saw a long, wispy beard on a pointed chin, long flowing hair that hid much of a gaunt face, and where the eyes should have been, only a pair of dark glasses. Helplessly, she stared into the two dark circles and saw her own puzzled reflections staring back at her.

"Oh." She recovered herself with a nervous laugh. "You scared me. I didn't even see you coming."

"One honey muffin. Please," the voice said again. It was soft, like his skin, almost a whisper, and Trish had the fleeting thought that if she heard the voice over a telephone, she probably wouldn't be able to guess its gender at all.

Flashing a quick smile at the expressionless face, she reached down into one of the bins, her hand closing around the largest muffin in the batch. It was heart-shaped, drizzled with golden honey on top, and as she slipped it into a bag, some of the honey came off onto her fingertips, causing the sack to stick to her hand.

"Oh, wait. Here. Sorry." She laughed, trying to pull her hand free, reaching at the same time for a cloth. As she glanced back at him, her laugh caught in her throat at the strange smile on his face.

"You have lovely hands," he said softly. "So small. Petite." He was silent a moment, yet she could feel his eyes studying her hands, even as she tried to wrap them in the cloth. "The way that honey looks on your fingers . . . one could almost . . . taste it."

Nervously, Trish looked around the cubicle. Bethany was nowhere to be seen, and no other customers were approaching her counter. Hastily cleaning her hands, she rang up the sale and tried to make her voice authoritative.

"One eighty-nine, please."

His palm still lay flat on the countertop, the money still waiting to be taken. For one instant, Trish was almost afraid to touch it, then, giving herself a stern mental shake, she jerked it from his hand and began pulling change from the register.

"Three eleven, sir," she said briskly.

She counted it out onto the counter. It lay there for a long moment, then slowly his hand shifted, the fingers curling around the bills and coins, sliding them to the edge, sliding them into the pocket of his coat.

"Thank you," he whispered. "You'll see me again."

He started away, paused for a second, then turned slightly, looking back at her over his shoulder. Trish busied herself with the baker's rack at the rear of the stand, and when she finally turned around again, he had gone.

Immensely relieved, she sagged back against the wall, putting one hand to her heart. There'd been something so unsettling about that man—something so weirdly different—and she suddenly realized she was shaking. She was sure he'd left The Eatery, yet she could still see him—the dark, blank circles where his eyes should have been, the unusual ash-gray color of his hair and beard.

Just a crazy, she argued to herself. *Just your usual eccentric customer.*

Nothing to get upset about. . . .

2

So do you think it was the same guy?" Trish persisted. She watched as Nita sorted an armload of sweaters, and wished for the hundredth time that she could have found a job in a clothing store like this one.

"I don't know—it sounds like it could be." Nita shook her head and chuckled. "How totally *weird!* You just never know these days who's going to be behind a newspaper!"

"It's not funny, Nita. He was really creepy." Trish frowned and glanced at her watch. "If you're going to eat dinner with me, then come on. I don't have all night. Bethany's watching me like a hawk."

"Don't you just love this new display I did?" Nita steered her toward a counter, beaming proudly. "All these old-fashioned paperweights with these wonderful patterns all over them? Don't you think they go with these new scarves?"

"Well," Trish said doubtfully, "I guess . . ."

"Well, I mean, they don't match *exactly,*" Nita said, sounding indignant. "It's—you know—art."

"I think it's nice," Trish said quickly. "Now can we go eat?"

"We have to get Imogene first," Nita reminded her. "If we can tear her away from her stupid bookstore. I think she's the only one in the whole *universe* who actually eats, sleeps, and breathes her work."

"Imogene likes everything," Trish reminded her, smiling fondly.

Imogene and Nita were twins, but no one would ever have guessed it. Nita had a tall, willowy dancer's frame and a classical sort of beauty, while Imogene was straight and prim, with mousey brown hair and glasses that looked too big for her face. The three of them had been inseparable since fourth grade, doing everything together—and now as seniors in high school, they were still the very best of friends. While The Eatery was located in the center section of the mall on the main floor, The Latest Trend, where Nita worked, was on the second level, with Imogene working directly opposite in the bookstore. Now, while Nita finished up with her sweaters, Trish walked to the entrance and waved as Imogene wandered out of the bookstore with her nose in a magazine.

"Hi," Trish greeted her as they sat down together on a bench to wait for Nita.

"Hi, yourself." Imogene always reminded Trish of a little wise old owl-woman, with her round glasses and her equally round stare. "There's more to this mall than meets the eye."

Trish looked startled. "Why do you say that?"

"I have a theory—" Imogene began, then looked up as Nita stopped beside them with a groan.

"You *always* have a theory about something. And

right now I can't take a single one of your theories on an empty stomach."

"Mexican?" Trish suggested. Their favorite fast food was located at the farthest end of The Eatery and the farthest away from Bethany's watchful eye.

"It's the spice of life." Imogene shrugged, falling into step behind them.

"It's the *only* spice in your life," Nita threw back. "Honestly, Imogene, I'm *so* glad we're not identical."

"But you're still not taking me seriously," Trish broke in, referring back to their conversation at the store. "That guy. I'm telling you, he was *really* strange."

"What guy?" Imogene asked.

"Oh, some weirdo hitting on Trish and her muffins," Nita chuckled. "Look, there are *lots* of crazies at this mall." She waved her hand airily, indicating the crowds around them. "They're *harmless!* I mean, this place is *full* of people. Nobody's going to try anything weird with all these other people around."

"That's not necessarily so," Imogene spoke up. "Actually, it's the perfect place for someone to try something weird. One could easily get lost in the masses."

"You go." Nita shoved her good-naturedly. "You go get lost in the masses. Please."

Imogene ignored her. She stared solemnly at Trish, who looked back with a tolerant smile as the girl continued. "There's always something going on at a mall, you know. And especially this mall."

"Okay," Nita sighed. "You don't have to go on sounding so mysterious, you've hooked my curiosity. Why especially *this* mall?"

"Well, surely you can see for yourself, this mall is not like other malls," Imogene said matter-of-factly.

"Because it's the oldest mall in the whole state?" Nita tried to keep a straight face. "Because it's the oldest mall to survive extinction and come out of the dark ages?"

"It's been renovated at least fifteen times over the years," Imogene went on, undaunted. "It's been built over time and time again without any real architectural pattern or design."

"It is a mess," Trish agreed, looking around as they walked. "But that's what I like about it. I think that's what *everyone* likes about this old place. It's got a kind of charm that no other mall has. None of the new ones, anyway."

"Macabre charm," Imogene clarified. "I'd be willing to bet there are so many tunnels and hallways and passages built on and added to over the years, there's probably no one still living who knows about all of them."

"Ooh," Nita shuddered deliciously. "I like it."

"I don't." Trish frowned. "And why did you have to bring all that up anyway, Imogene?"

"Because I've been hearing the rumors again," Imogene said stubbornly.

"What rumors?" Trish asked.

"If you mean about what happened at my store last night—" Nita began, but Imogene cut her off.

"I mean the shoplifting."

This time Nita and Trish echoed together. "Shoplifting?"

Imogene nodded. "Things are disappearing. All over the mall."

Nita burst into laughter. "Come on, Imogene, things are *always* being shoplifted around here—you call that news? Tell me something *really* juicy."

"But that's not the point," Imogene went on calmly.

"Okay," Trish conceded, "what *is* the point?"

"The point is that none of the alarm systems are going off."

"Those dinky little alarm systems aren't worth anything, and you know it," Nita chuckled. "I bet we lose *hundreds* of dollars of stuff every month, just in *our* little place."

"No," Imogene continued, "even the new systems —the more sophisticated systems they've tried out in the department stores. They're not catching these things being stolen."

"Well, what *really* makes me mad is that *someone* out there is ripping off all these *wonderful* clothes and *I* have to *pay* for the ones I want!" Nita rolled her eyes.

"Not just clothing," Imogene informed her. "Lots of other things. Like kitchen equipment, for example."

"What kind of kitchen equipment?" Trish glanced at her.

"Dishes. Gourmet foodstuffs. Even bottles of wine and ice picks."

"Someone's throwing a hell of a party," Nita chuckled. "Wish they'd invite *me.*"

"Linens," Imogene went on calmly. "Pillows . . . blankets . . . perfumes. Even furniture."

"Furniture?" Trish laughed. "How can anyone sneak out a piece of furniture?"

"And books," Imogene sounded indignant. "From *my* bookstore."

"So," Nita sighed, "what are you saying?"

"I have a theory—"

"I have hunger pains!" Nita threw up her hands. *"Enough,* already! Give me some money, Imogene—I left my purse in the store."

"How convenient." Trish gave Nita a reproachful

look as Imogene obligingly dug into her bag and handed her sister some bills.

"Well, at least she's good for something." Nita grinned shamelessly and led the way to an empty table.

While Nita and Imogene went off to get the food, Trish sat and saved their places, letting her eyes wander idly around the busy Eatery. There was every kind of meal for sale here—from junk food to health food, from pastry to salad bars to ethnic temptations —and the huge area was always filled with people, always noisy with conversation and laughter and the rattle and clatter of dishes. As Trish's gaze swept over each food stand, it finally came to rest on Pizza Park, and she saw Storm Reynolds leaning lazily across the counter, waiting on a customer.

She could watch him now—could look at him from this distance without worrying that he saw her. He was writing down an order and laughing, and from time to time he stopped to point at the wall behind him, where the menu was posted. As Trish recalled his wink at her earlier, a shy smile came to her lips, but then it quickly faded as another face replaced Storm's in her mind. With a quick intake of breath, she stiffened in her chair and redirected her stare across The Eatery again, seeking out long ash-gray hair and dark glasses. *He could still be here, you know . . . sitting anywhere . . . watching anywhere. . . .*

"But he's not," she said out loud to herself, and she grabbed the seat of her chair with both hands, trying to get a grip on her fears. "He's not anywhere—he was just some weirdo who was hanging around the mall, but now he's gone, and you're never going to see him again."

"You're talking to yourself." Nita's voice sounded

so close beside her that Trish jumped. "You're getting more and more like Imogene every day." As Trish took the tray her friend handed her, Nita glanced around slyly. "I bet *I* know what you were dreaming about—*who* you were dreaming about." Her face grew dreamy and she nodded toward Pizza Park.

"Don't be ridiculous," Trish sighed. "He's probably got ten dozen girlfriends."

"But he winked at *you.*"

"Which proves he's just a huge flirt. A flirt and probably fickle. A flirt and fickle and not to be trusted."

"A man," Imogene clarified soberly, and Nita looked amused.

"Oh, listen to Imogene, the expert," she teased. "Okay, then, let's pick someone out for Imogene, Trish. Someone in The Eatery. Who should it be?"

Imogene looked more bored than annoyed. "Don't you have anything more intelligent to do?"

"Look—*there* he is!" Nita grabbed Trish's sleeve and shook it excitedly. "There he *is*—Imogene's *guy!* The man of her *dreams!*"

As Trish followed the point of Nita's finger, she saw a young man standing at one of the trash cans, dumping in food scraps from a pile of dirty trays.

"Oh, stop it, Nita—" Trish began, but Nita broke in again.

"*Look* at him, Trish—he's just her *type!* Five foot—what—ten? Or maybe *six* whole feet if he stood up straight! Long hair—combed back—or is it *greased* back? Jeans with holes—oh, sorry—maybe he's trying to be stylish—and a T-shirt with something . . ." Nita squinted her eyes, trying to see. ". . . *something* written on the front—wait a minute—yes—*yes*—okay, now we know he *loves* rock music! And the *sexiest* combat boots—don't you think so, Trish? Oh—and that denim jacket with the sleeves cut off—the absolutely *perfect* touch!"

Trish took a bite of her taco and glanced over at Imogene. "I think his name is Wyatt. I always see him working around here, but I don't really know anything about him. He kind of keeps to himself."

"Wyatt," Nita crooned. "The absolutely *perfect* name!"

"Actually," Imogene said stiffly, "I think he's rather nice-looking."

Nita's mouth fell open. Trish burst into laughter.

"So there you are, Nita. You're a better matchmaker than you thought!"

They kept watching as Wyatt scraped the last of his trays, picked up the whole stack, then started past their table. Trish glanced at Nita and saw the impish look on her face, but before Trish could say a word, Nita shoved her chair back, ramming Wyatt in the stomach. There was a resounding crash as the trays bounced all over the floor, and people in the food stands began to cheer.

"Oh, my gosh!" Nita exclaimed, looking up wide-eyed at Wyatt. "Where did *you* come from!"

Imogene put her head down on her arms and groaned. Trish scooted her chair back, trying to decide whether to help or just die of embarrassment.

"I'm so sorry I *hit* you!" Nita insisted. She reached out toward Wyatt's midsection, hesitated, then pressed her hand lightly against the front of his shirt. "I *really* didn't notice you there!"

Wyatt stared at her. He gazed down at the mess on the floor. He looked back at Nita again, his face bland.

"Yeah. It's so hard to *see* me with all this stuff I'm carrying."

Calmly he took hold of her hand and pushed it away. Trish started to laugh, but caught herself in time. She glanced quickly at Nita and saw the girl's mouth open in surprise.

"Well . . . I—I *said* I was sorry." Nita tried to recover herself, lowering her long lashes in her most heart-melting way.

Wyatt didn't seem to notice.

"I'm Nita," she added, almost desperately. "And—and this is my friend Trish. And this is my sister Imogene—"

She broke off, amazed, as Wyatt walked off, leaving the trays scattered around their table.

Trish and Imogene stared, openmouthed, then both of them burst into fits of laughter.

"Well, I don't know what *you* two are getting so hysterical about," Nita said indignantly. "I thought that was very *rude* of him!"

"Oh—" Trish nodded. "And you crippling the poor guy—*nothing* rude there!"

"Well, he didn't have to be like that." Nita pouted. She stared at Wyatt's retreating back, then rested her chin in her hands. "Hmmm . . . he's a challenge, all right."

"Did I miss something here?" Trish laughed again. "Weren't you trying to grab him for Imogene?"

"Forget it," Imogene said matter-of-factly. "He made the mistake of ignoring her. Now the poor guy doesn't know what he's in for."

"Well, really." Nita sat up straighter, frowning. "How hard could this turn out to be? I mean—well—*look* at him!"

"I did." Trish stood and gathered up the remains of her dinner to throw away. "He looked pretty cute to me."

"And intelligent," Imogene added, straight-faced.

"*That* thing!" Nita yelped. "*Him?* Excuse me, but I think you must have him mixed up with somebody else. Like someone with a brain, maybe?"

"That was terrible of you," Trish scolded, dumping her trash in the litter can. "You deserved just what you got. I don't feel sorry for you one bit."

"Well, *all* I was trying to do was get Imogene a date," Nita defended herself. "I mean, *nobody's* going to ask her out if she just sits there with her *face* on the table!" She tossed her tray on top of the can and gave Imogene a patronizing look. "Imogene, you've just *got* to get yourself some kind of *life* or something."

"Well, really, right *now* what I've got to do is get back to work," Imogene sighed, and got up. "And thank *you*, Nita, for the entertainment."

As Trish started back to the muffin stand, she couldn't resist one last glance toward Pizza Park. She could see Storm talking to a sullen Wyatt and laughing uproariously, and she chuckled to herself, guessing that he'd watched the whole scene.

"You've got a message," Bethany greeted her crossly, as Trish got back to work. "And from now on, when I say dinner is half an hour, that doesn't mean three minutes after."

Trish nodded mutely, puzzled about what might be waiting for her, and was surprised when Bethany handed her a piece of paper.

"What is it?" she asked, but Bethany was already disappearing into the back room.

"I don't know. Something about your car. Somebody hit it or something."

"Hit it? In the parking lot?" Trish's heart sank. "Well . . . what should I do?"

"He said for you to go take a look at it," Bethany

grumbled. "He has to make out a report or something."

Trish unfolded the scrap of paper and saw a curt message scrawled there. It noted the make and model of her car and instructed her to notify the security office after checking out the damage. Irritated, she grabbed her jacket and hurried through the mall to the north exit. Employee parking was in the farthest lot from the building, and she didn't relish the idea of walking all that way in the cold, then having to come all the way back again.

"Just my luck," she muttered, starting her trek across the huge parking area. "I just get that stupid car out of the shop, and someone mangles it."

She walked briskly, hugging herself against the cold, glancing up from time to time at the round October moon glowing behind wispy clouds. Even though the parking lots were dotted with streetlamps, less than half of them ever worked, and she'd made it a practice to always carry a pocket flashlight in her coat. It took nearly five minutes to reach the employee lot. She remembered she'd found a spot near a pay phone that afternoon, and as she finally spotted her old Mustang, she began to run, already fumbling in her pockets for her light.

To her surprise, there didn't seem to be anything wrong with the car at all.

Stopping a few feet away, Trish surveyed it carefully, letting her eyes wander over every inch of the outside, searching for some sign of damage. The car looked fine—just as she'd left it that afternoon when she came to work. Puzzled, she walked slowly all around it, playing her flashlight over the hood—the sides—the trunk—the tires—then came back to her original spot, shaking her head. *There must be some*

*mistake . . . it must have been someone else's car . . .
they got the license plates mixed up somehow. . . .*

More annoyed now than bewildered, Trish backed
away from the car and turned to go.

And when the pay phone suddenly rang, shattering
the darkness with its shrill scream, she froze there,
watching it with her mouth open, unable to believe
what she was hearing.

The phone rang.

And rang.

Trish stood there, staring, the cold seeping through
her jacket . . . through her skin . . . deep, deep into
her veins.

*It must be for somebody . . . somebody who's sup-
posed to be here right now at this exact moment . . .
only they're not here and it might be important . . .
and whoever is calling will just keep waiting and
waiting and nobody might ever come. . . .*

Trish walked over to the phone. She reached out
and took the receiver, lifting it slowly to her ear.

"Hello, Trish," the voice said. It was a whisper . . .
soft and familiar . . .yet strangely unreal. . . .

It sounded like dark reflections and ash-gray
shadows. . . .

"I'm eating the muffin," he said. "It tastes just like
you."

3

As Trish raced back into the mall, she spotted a security guard near the information booth and stopped breathlessly in front of him.

"You've got to help me!" she pleaded.

She saw the tired look of suspicion on his face, and the way his hand automatically went for the walkie-talkie at his belt.

"The—the phone out in the parking lot—" She was gasping for breath, trying to get the words out, trying to stop shaking. She'd run all the way from her car, and she felt frozen, her words tumbling uselessly, making no sense at all.

"Take it easy now, Miss. What's the problem?" The guard was using his most patronizing tone of voice. "You say the pay phone isn't working in the parking lot? Well, that's not our problem. You'll have to contact the telephone company and—"

"No—no—" In spite of her best efforts to be rational, Trish reached out and tugged at his sleeve. He stepped away and firmly but gently removed her hand.

"Okay, now, just calm down a minute."

"No, my car—someone ran into my car—but—"

"You need a tow truck? You can call one from here." He moved toward the information booth, and Trish stepped quickly in front of him.

"No, you don't understand—you're not *listening!*" she said, more frustrated by the second. She saw the growing annoyance in his eyes, but she rushed on. "They said someone hit my car—only *no* one hit my car—but the *phone* started ringing—the *pay phone* by my *car*—"

"Okay, hold on. You say the pay phone by your car—the pay phone in the parking lot?"

"Yes, yes, that's right." Trish was nodding frantically, hopeful that at last something was beginning to get through to him. "See—it started ringing—and so I answered it—"

"You answered the phone in the parking lot."

"Yes! Only it was horrible—this guy—I saw him in the mall earlier this evening—it was *him* on the phone—"

"*Who* was on the phone? A guy you know?"

"No—I don't really know him—"

"But he knows you. So he called you on the phone in the parking lot."

"No! I mean, *yes!* I mean—" Trish broke off abruptly, seeing the cold mask of indifference settle over her face. He folded his arms across his chest and glared at her.

"Look, girlie, I don't have time for all these pranks

you *kids* think it's so much fun to play on each other—"

"You think—" Trish sputtered. "You think this is a—a—*joke!* Well, it's not! And *I'm* not your girlie!"

"Don't fool around with me, kid—you're liable to ruin my good mood." He glowered at her. "And tell your boyfriend to grow up and quit playing stupid tricks, huh?"

As Trish stared in disbelief, he turned on his heel and walked away.

It took her several minutes to recover, she was so angry. Standing there while the busy throngs of shoppers jostled around her, she suddenly had the eerie sensation of being someone else—someone in a movie—and the real Trish was just standing there watching the other Trish's frustration and rage. *This can't be happening to me. Things like this don't happen to real people in real life.*

She began to walk, mechanically, vaguely aware that she had to get back to work before she got in worse trouble. *Prank!* She could still hear the phone ringing—shrill—shrill—*insistent*—could still hear that voice. *He knew my name—he knew I'd be there—he knew I'd answer. . . .*

"Oh, God!" Trish stopped and covered her face with her hands, and then immediately pitched forward as someone rammed her from behind.

"Hey, are you okay?"

As strong hands caught her by the shoulders and steadied her, she managed to twist around and look up—right into Storm Reynolds's dark blue eyes.

"Well, hi there." He grinned. "How's the muffin business?"

In spite of her present frame of mind, Trish could

feel her cheeks turning red, and she quickly looked away.

"Oh—oh, hi. I—I didn't know that was you."

"Or you'd have gotten out of my way, right?" He had a cute grin, teasing and sexy at the same time, and a habit of cocking his head a little to one side when he spoke.

"I—I guess I wasn't paying much attention," Trish said lamely.

"No, *I'm* the one who wasn't paying attention. It's a bad habit of mine." His grin widened. "Although sometimes bad habits pay off."

His blue eyes held hers for a moment, and with an effort she forced herself to look away again.

"Are you . . . on break?" she finally asked, and he nodded.

"Getting some exercise. Care to join me?"

"I—" *I'd love to.* "I guess not—I mean—I have to get back to work."

"You feel cold. You been outside?"

She nodded. Again she heard the ringing of the telephone and the whisper of that horrible voice. She stammered in confusion. "I . . . I thought my car'd been hit."

Storm was watching her, his face puzzled. "You thought? You weren't in it?"

"No . . . that is . . . someone left me a *message* saying it'd been hit. But when I got there, it didn't look like anything had happened to it."

"You sure? Do you want to check it again? I'll be glad to go with you."

Trish started to agree, then stopped herself. He was practically a total stranger—she didn't even know him that well. How could she ever explain to him what had happened out there? He'd never believe her, and he'd probably think she was completely crazy. *Definitely not something that'll make a good first impression.*

"No," she said at last. "I mean . . . no, I'm sure it hasn't been hit. Someone must have gotten it mixed up with another car."

He was still staring at her. He nodded slowly. "Well . . . that's good, isn't it?"

"Yes." She was staring out at the main walkway, the milling throngs of people, the bright lights. What had just happened to her out there *couldn't* have been real—it was too incredible. No wonder that guard hadn't taken her seriously.

"What's your name?" he asked, smiling.

"What?" She snapped back to the present, conscious now of his eyes upon her.

"I'd like to know your name," he said. "Is that okay?"

"Trish. Trish Somerfield."

He nodded. "I see you when you're working. I don't know if you ever noticed, but our stands are right across from each other."

As if I hadn't noticed. "I . . . yes . . . I've seen you," she said lamely.

"My name's Storm Reynolds."

I know your name. I'm sure every girl in the mall knows your name.

"You haven't been working here long, have you? Let me guess." He thought a moment, his eyes twinkling. "Five days. Five days exactly."

"Yes," Trish nodded, startled.

"Or should I say five nights. You don't work days. You come in the afternoon and work till closing."

"I . . . that's right."

"You look surprised." He squeezed her shoulders,

27

and that wonderful grin played at the corners of his mouth. "I always notice the really *important* things."

Trish could feel her cheeks growing warm again, and she lowered her head.

"Well . . ." Storm took a quick glance around them and gave her a playful shake. "Do you realize we're still standing here holding up traffic? What do you say I walk you back to work?"

"Oh . . . really . . . you don't have to—"

"I know I don't have to." His look was mildly reproachful. "It's the least I can do for running you over."

Before she could answer, his hands slid down her shoulders onto her arms, and he turned her around, guiding her through the crowds. Trish was almost relieved that he was steering her—her head was spinning so fast, she could hardly concentrate on where she was going.

As they reached The Eatery, Trish could see the long line of people waiting at the muffin counter. She could also see Bethany standing at the register watching her with a stony expression. She didn't realize she'd even reacted, but suddenly Storm stopped and gently pulled her back against him.

"Problem?"

"No," she said quickly. "It's . . . nothing."

"It must be something. Bodies don't go that tense for no reason."

"It's my manager," Trish said almost apologetically. "We . . . we don't get along very well."

"Hey." He leaned down, and she could feel his breath on her ear. "Don't worry. It'll be okay."

His hands lingered a moment longer on her arms, then he suddenly turned and went back to his booth.

Trish steeled herself for an attack as she got behind the counter, but Bethany showed remarkable control.

"How's your car?" she asked stiffly.

"It was . . . okay," Trish murmured.

"Okay? I'd hate to guess how long it would have taken, if it *hadn't* been okay."

Trish said nothing, only stepped up to the front and began filling orders. At least for a while this was something mechanical she could do to keep from thinking—something pleasant she could put into the dark, confused spaces of her mind.

Yet somehow the customers didn't seem so friendly to her tonight, pressing so close against the booth, pointing and pushing, unable to make up their minds. . . .

And as she listened to their clamoring all around her, she was suddenly terrified that a soft, strange voice would whisper her name from the crowd.

4

You *are* kidding, aren't you?"

Nita stared at Trish with wide eyes, her head shaking slowly from side to side.

"Please, Trish, tell me you're just trying to scare me—"

"Nita, why on earth would I kid about something like *this!*"

"Because it's time to close up, and we have to walk out to the parking lot together, and you *know* how I *hate* things like that!" Nita glanced up at the clock, then back at Trish. Trish stared down at the floor and wrapped her arms tightly around her chest.

"I'm not kidding, Nita. The phone in the parking lot was really ringing, and I really picked it up, and the voice really said what I told you he said."

"That's so perverted," Nita groaned. "So you think it was the muffin man?"

"Well, who else could it have been?" Trish sighed.

She wandered over to a rack of blouses, sorting through them disinterestedly. "He knew my name, Nita," she said softly. "He must have given that message to Bethany, and then he knew when I got to my car. He knew the number on that phone, and somehow . . . he knew I'd pick it up."

"Oh, Trish," Nita began, but Trish angrily cut her off.

"Why'd I ever pick up that *phone!* It was a *stupid* thing to do—I can't *believe* I was so stupid!"

"You weren't stupid," Nita defended her, smiling a little. "Trish, when a phone rings out in the middle of nowhere, it's so unexpected—I don't know—I probably would have thought someone was in trouble or . . ."

"It was stupid," Trish murmured. She walked to the doors at the front of the store and stared out onto the main walkway. Shoppers were hurrying back and forth in a steady stream, heading for the parking lots, and already the other shops along the corridor were closing up for the night.

"Are you going to be long?" she asked absently, and felt Nita's hand on her shoulder.

"I hope not. Imogene's going to the library to do some studying, so she already got a ride with someone. And these stupid girls came in at the last minute, and they're still in the dressing rooms."

"Can't you make them leave?"

"I've only told them to about a hundred times already," Nita chuckled, but Trish didn't join in. "Look—we have to tell someone about this."

"Oh, no one's going to believe this, Nita. I told that guard out there and he looked at me like I was some kind of delinquent!" Frustrated, Trish plopped down in a chair and glowered. "I know it was a dumb thing to do, but I did it. Now I have to figure out what to do next. What if he calls me again?"

"Now, how's he going to do that?" Nita put her hands on her hips, looking dismayed. "Like you're going to answer phones in the parking lot from now on? Look, Trish, it was probably just a one-shot deal. This guy just wanted to do something perverted, and he did it and he got his thrills, so now he'll just go on his merry way. That's usually how weirdos like that operate, isn't it? They're not really dangerous, are they?"

"It was just so calculating," Trish muttered, more to herself than to Nita. "He had to have known when I was there so he could make the call. So where was *he?*"

"I'm not sure you can see all the way to the employee lot from the mall," Nita said doubtfully. "Maybe he was timing you. That's possible, isn't it? He could have been in The Eatery and saw you leave, so he took a chance that when he called, you'd be at your car."

Trish gave a reluctant nod. "It's possible, I guess. Unless he was closer. Maybe he was in a car somewhere at another pay phone in another part of the parking lot. He could have seen me from there, I guess."

"Or timed you again," Nita thought aloud.

"Or maybe he was in a car and he had a car phone."

Nita shuddered. "And anyone could get that pay phone number. So he did it as a sick joke and now you'll never hear from him again."

"I hope you're right." Trish sighed.

"But I still think we should tell the police," Nita persisted. "If there's some sicko running around the mall, they should know about it, so they can do something."

"But I sounded like an idiot," Trish said unhappily. "I mean . . . when I heard myself telling that guard what happened out there. Who's going to believe a story like that? Would *you?* If you didn't know me?"

Nita gave her an understanding smile. "Well . . . it is pretty hard to believe, I guess. I see what you mean."

"And how did he know my name?" Trish sighed again. She put one hand to her temple, rubbing the headache that was. beginning there. "He said my *name,* Nita—how did he know my *name?"*

"He could have asked around at The Eatery. For that matter, anyone could probably find out who works here if they went to the main office—"

"Nita . . ." Trish stood up slowly, her eyes widening. "Are you thinking what I'm thinking? Maybe he *works* here?"

Nita stared at her a moment, then shook her head. "I don't know. . . . If we're talking about the guy behind the newspaper, I don't remember *anyone* around here who looks like that."

"Are you sure? Think hard."

"But there're so many shops here—so many employees," Nita shrugged helplessly. "And there must be thousands—*hundreds* of thousands—of shoppers. Trish, you'll probably never know who this guy is. I really have a feeling it was a one-shot thing, like I said before. Once he saw you run back to the mall, and he figured he'd scared you to death, he probably took off. He's probably going to be at some other mall tomorrow trying to scare some other girl out of her mind."

Trish nodded, not entirely convinced. "Can we go now, Nita? I'd really like to get home."

"Is your mom still out of town?" Nita looked sympathetic.

"Yes, she's still on that stupid business trip flying

around Europe somewhere," Trish said gloomily. "You're so lucky your parents aren't divorced. And that you have a *normal* mother instead of a business executive!"

"That's funny." Nita smiled. "I always wanted a mom like yours. Yours is a lot more glamorous. Plus the fact that you have all that *wonderful* privacy." She gave a wistful sigh, and Trish couldn't help chuckling.

"It's not privacy, Nita. It's total solitude. Not real fun when you've just gotten a crazy phone call in a parking lot."

"You know you can always stay with us." Nita gave her a hug, and Trish hugged her back gratefully.

"I know. But it's only for the rest of the week. And I don't want to wear out my welcome until I'm sure I'm *really* being terrorized!"

It was meant to be a joke, but neither of them laughed.

Nita glanced once more at the clock, then shouted toward the back of the store, where the dressing rooms were located. "Come on, you all have to leave! I'm closing up the store now!"

Trish glanced around and suddenly realized that Nita seemed to be the only one working.

"Are you by yourself tonight?"

"Well, Freida was supposed to be with me, but obviously nobody knew she was planning a trip." Nita made a face. "I still have to clean up, so I'll be a while. See anything you want to try on? We got some new stuff in today."

Trish got up and wandered around the store, sorting absentmindedly through racks of clothes, picking up sweaters, putting them down again. Normally she would have jumped at the chance to have first pick at the new selections, but her heart just wasn't in it. She could hear Nita running the vacuum cleaner, and the muffled giggles coming from the girls in the dressing rooms. From the record store next door the driving beat of a rock band reverberated through the walls. Pausing beside a display of new dresses, Trish flipped quickly through the hangers, then drew her breath in slowly.

She'd never seen such a beautiful dress. Long and flowing, it was all white satin and lace, like a gauzy cloud, with delicate trimmings of ribbons and velvet. Holding it at arm's length, she ran a finger carefully along the low-cut neckline, the tiny row of pearl buttons down the front, the soft, full skirt. *A princess might have worn this,* she found herself thinking, and she smiled, feeling silly for her own romantic notions. *Some long-ago princess in some passionate legend with some wildly happy ending. . . .*

"It's you," Nita declared, stopping beside her and nodding emphatically. "It is. Try it on."

Trish hesitated, read the price tag, started to put it back.

"You've got to be kidding. As if I could ever afford such a—"

"Try it *on!*" Nita grabbed the dress from her and began shoving her toward the fitting rooms. "It's part of our new Purely Passion line—and not just *anyone* could wear this wonderfully sweet, and very naughty, dress! Go on—you've got time! I want to see how it looks on you!"

As Trish started in to the dressing rooms, she met the other girls coming out. Pushing and still giggling, they converged upon the front counter with armloads of clothes, and Trish guessed Nita would be busy a good fifteen minutes more just ringing them up. *Well, why not? I can dream, can't I?*

The girls had left the dressing rooms in total disarray, and as Trish made her way along the short passage, stepping clumsily over piles of clothes, she discovered that the last two cubicles were the only ones clean. It was a small area—just the hallway with a full-length mirror at the end of it and five tiny stalls branching off on each side. The stalls had no doors, but rather bright blue curtains which pulled together and fell about a foot short of the blue-carpeted floor. Trish hung her dress on the wall and started to close her curtains, then stopped, chuckling to herself. There was nobody else here, and the mirror was right outside. She decided to leave the curtains open.

Again she ran one hand slowly over the dress, loving the flow of it beneath her fingertips. Anyone who wore a dress as beautiful as this couldn't help but *feel* beautiful, she thought—and it'd been a long time since she'd felt that way. Nita was the one who got all the dates—and Imogene was the member of all the clubs at school—but Trish was just Trish. *Boring and unpopular.* And nice, she reminded herself—everyone was always reminding her how wonderfully nice she was. But being nice still didn't make her less boring or any more popular—*at least with the guys. . . .*

Sighing, she pulled her sweater up over her head and shook out her tangled hair. There were no more hooks on the wall, so she dropped the sweater onto the floor in the corner. She unzipped her pants and slid them down her hips, then paused a moment to kick off her shoes. As she bent over to lift her jeans from around her bare feet, a cold chill suddenly snaked across her legs, and startled, she straightened up and peered out into the hall.

"Nita? Is that you?"

There was no one in the aisle. Empty dressing rooms gaped around her, and she slowly stepped back into the stall.

"Nita? Come on, are you trying to scare me?"

And yet she could hear the soft murmur of voices from the main part of the store . . . Nita's unmistakable laugh from the front counter.

You're imagining things . . . that whole thing with the muffin man . . . you're just paranoid. . . .

Taking a deep breath, Trish slipped the dress from its hanger and stepped out into the hall. There was more room out here, and she didn't like the feeling of being cornered in that tiny cubicle. She stood and looked at herself in the mirror, examining her body with a critical eye. It wasn't that she didn't have a shape—Nita was always telling her she had great curves in all the right places—it was that she always felt stupid letting anyone see her. Bulky clothes made her feel comfortable—hidden and safe.

Safe. . . .

Uneasily, Trish glanced behind her, down the short expanse of hallway. She knew she was being silly, but it was almost as if someone else had suddenly come into the dressing area with her . . . as if somehow she'd heard a quiet footstep . . . sensed some stealthy, hidden movement.

Trish shivered and turned back to the mirror. She pulled the dress down over her head and began fastening the delicate pearls along the bodice. She could hardly believe how it made her look—all softness and light, the curves of her breasts just showing above the daring neckline. As she took a step back, for once she couldn't help smiling at her own reflection.

And then she felt it again.

The icy stream of air across the floor . . . across her bare feet . . . and as she lowered her eyes, she saw the hem of her skirt rustle softly, as if some invisible hand had touched it.

Gasping, she jerked her head up, and suddenly she *knew* what it was that had alarmed her before—that strange, unknown something that had frightened her and made her feel that she wasn't alone in these dressing rooms.

Eyes.

She knew it now, just as surely as she was standing here, that she really *wasn't* alone. That someone— somewhere—was watching her—and *had* been watching her for some time.

With a choked cry, Trish gathered up her skirt and ran.

5

Nita!"

As Trish flew out of the dressing rooms, she saw Nita standing in the store entrance. The last shoppers were just leaving, and as Nita hurriedly closed and locked the doors, Trish reached her at last, grabbing her in a panic.

"What?" Nita looked frightened now, and she was trying to pull out of Trish's grasp, trying to grab Trish around the shoulders. "What *is* it? What's the—"

"There's someone in there, Nita."

"What? Where?"

"There—in the dressing rooms—watching me—"

"Watching you? What are you talking about?"

"Someone's *in* there! I saw—"

"Oh, my God, are you *sure?"* Nita gave Trish a firm shake. "Stop it, Trish! Calm down! What—"

"I'm not *kidding*—someone—"

"That's impossible." Nita released her and started back through the store. "I was just *back* there!"

"No, Nita, don't go!" Trish caught her again and jerked her back. "You don't know what might happen —call security—*please!*"

Again Nita broke free and stalked determinedly toward the dressing area.

"Trish, I've been standing right there by the door the whole time! No one was in the dressing rooms except those girls—and then you! I know I'm right! I was *back* there!"

"I don't care—please don't go back there now—"

"What was it?" Nita was still heading toward the rear of the store, with Trish right on her heels. "What did you see?"

"I—nothing!" Trish burst out. She saw Nita stop ahead of her, saw her bewildered expression as she looked back over her shoulder.

"You saw . . . nothing?"

"Nita, this is no time to be technical! I know someone was watching me! I felt these eyes—staring at me! I felt this—this—draft—and—"

"Draft?" Nita repeated dumbly. "You felt a . . . draft?"

"Oh, I know it sounds crazy—"

"You're right," Nita sighed. "It does. It sounds crazy." She marched up to the doorway that led to the dressing rooms and stopped again, putting her hands on her hips. "Hello!" she shouted. "Is anyone back there? Joke's over, whoever you are—do you hear me? Security's on their way—so get out of there— *now!*"

Trish huddled against her and they listened. The silence went on and on. Nita glanced at Trish and frowned.

"Maybe he's deaf."

"That's not funny. I *didn't* imagine it."

"I didn't say you imagined it. Come on."

"No—" Trish reached for her friend's arm, but Nita shook her off and started down the hallway, slapping at the curtains on either side.

"Look, they're all open—how could anyone be hiding back here?"

"The last one. On the left. The floor was ice cold. A breeze blew across my legs."

"Well, it's not cold now." Nita stooped down and ran her hand over the carpet. "I don't feel any kind of draft."

"But . . ." Trish looked helplessly at Nita. "*I* felt it!"

"Okay, so where were you standing?"

"In that room. And then in front of the mirror." Trish moved up alongside her friend and stared into the shiny surface of the glass. "That mirror, Nita—I don't know—something about it made me feel so creepy—"

"Your reflection," Nita joked, and then seeing the look on Trish's face was instantly contrite. "I'm sorry. I know you're really upset about this, but there's nothing here! It's only 'cause of what happened to you before, Trish—that muffin man and that weird call in the parking lot. You were back here by yourself, and you were probably thinking about it, and you started feeling all spooky about things."

"Well, then, why don't I feel it now?" Trish held up her arms in frustration, hardly even noticing when Nita leaned over and hugged her.

"Because *I'm* here, silly. Come on, stop worrying so much. It was a horrible joke, but he's gone now. Out of your life, whoever he was. Don't think about it anymore—you'll drive yourself crazy."

Trish sighed, turning around, surveying the hall and the rooms on either side. "I know you're right—I know none of this even makes sense—"

"I'm not saying I don't believe you. But if someone was really in here, then where are they now? I was standing right outside with all those other people. If there *had* been a prowler in here, he would have had to go right past all of us!"

Trish stood there, staring. She felt Nita put a hand on her arm and pat her gently.

"That dress looks really beautiful on you. I think you should buy it."

"With what?" Trish mumbled. "My looks?"

"No—your imagination." Nita grinned and reached out, forcing Trish to turn in a circle. "I mean it. Really. You look like a—a—queen or something grand like that."

"I just don't understand . . ."

"Don't think about it," Nita said firmly. "Get the dress."

"You know I can't afford it."

"Layaway?"

"Mom would kill me."

"I'll never tell."

Trish stole a last look in the mirror, saw her reflection there, like some magical stranger she'd never seen before.

"I . . . I do love it."

"I do, too."

"But . . . no." Firmly she shook her head, ignoring Nita's look of disappointment. "I better take it off before it enchants me or something."

"Okay, if you're going to be difficult. I'll just finish straightening up—"

"No!" Without even thinking, Trish reached out

and stopped her. "No . . . wait for me here. Just let me get dressed, and then I'll help you clean."

Nita grinned. "Sure. It'll take me two years just to pick up all these clothes around here anyway."

In half an hour the store was put to rights again, and the girls locked up, strolling slowly down the deserted corridors of the mall. There was only one exit open after closing time, and that was by the theaters, a convenience for moviegoers whose chosen features ran late into the night. Pulling on their jackets, the two friends stepped out into the night, lowering their faces against the biting wind. The pale yellow moon was almost invisible now in the starless sky, and fog had begun to drift in, making the streetlamps in the parking lots seem like tall, flickering candles.

"Want me to ride with you?" Nita asked sympathetically, pulling her gloves out of her pocket, blowing on her fingers. "I'm not sure you're in any shape to drive by yourself. We can go get something to eat, then you can bring me back to pick up my car later."

"Actually . . . yes." Trish gave her friend a grateful smile.

"This isn't like you." Nita frowned, shaking her head. "You're the one who's usually so sensible. You're the one who's usually so calm in a crisis."

"I know. It's a curse. Every once in a while I have to go a little berserk, just so you'll know I'm human." Trish laughed as Nita gave her a shove.

The massive parking lot stretched out before them, strangely surreal in the fog. As the girls pushed their way through the small crowd of late-night moviegoers, the cars began to thin out and finally disappeared altogether.

"I hope your heater works for a change." Nita gritted her teeth as a sudden blast of wind pelted them with dust and dead leaves. Beside her, Trish pressed closer and thrust her hands deep into her pockets.

"You know I can't make fancy promises. If it just gets us where we want to go, we'll be lucky."

"Where are you, anyway?"

"About as far away as you can park and still work here," Trish said grimly. "I was late getting here this afternoon—what can I say?"

She spotted her Mustang in the distance and unconsciously quickened her pace. Nita ran a little to keep up, stumbled, and promptly dropped her purse.

"Oh, no, there goes my makeup—all my credit cards—"

"Do you need some help?"

"No—no—never mind—I think I've got them all—"

"Here—use my flashlight. Are you sure?"

"Thanks—yes—just keep going. I'm doing fine."

Trish shook her head and kept on. "Just be glad *everything* didn't fall out of that suitcase of yours—we'd be here for the next month!"

"Well, I like to be prepared," Nita threw back, following her again. "You just never know what might happen that you should be ready for!"

"Too bad you don't have any hot dates in your purse." Trish laughed. "Or any automatic A's for that big English test we're having next week or—what's wrong now?"

Stopping, she glanced back, only to see that Nita had quit walking. The girl's head was raised slightly, as if she were listening to something Trish couldn't hear.

"Nita?" she said again, starting back. "What's—"

"Did you hear something?" Nita frowned.

"No. Like what?"

"I don't know." After another moment of listening, Nita made a disgusted sound in her throat and started walking again, taking Trish's elbow and dragging her along. "You've got me spooked tonight, Trish. I thought I heard . . . oh, never mind."

"What?" Trish repeated, exasperated. She was running a little, just to keep up with Nita's quick pace.

"Nothing. Footsteps. Or something like that. Nothing."

"Nothing?" Trish's eyes widened, and she glanced around as Nita urged her on. There were only a few cars now, watching them, like crouched animals in the fog might watch, dull headlights like blank, dead eyes. "Now *you're* imagining things."

"Yeah, I know. Come on."

Linking arms, they ran the rest of the way. As they neared the car at last, Trish found herself suddenly wondering if she'd remembered to lock it when she'd come to work that afternoon.

Footsteps. . . .

Nita couldn't have heard footsteps, Trish reasoned to herself . . . there was no place out here for anyone to hide . . . except in the fog. . . .

And then, suddenly, he was there.

Without warning, without the slightest sound, he was just *there,* materializing out of the fog like some phantom, standing motionless beside the car, while Trish's breath caught in her throat and she tried to call out, tried to *scream,* but no sound came—nothing at all—and Nita stared, paralyzed, the flashlight trembling in her hand.

"Someone's breaking into your car," Nita murmured.

And as Trish watched, the figure moved slowly toward them into the tiny pool of light.

45

6

Trish—"

From some remote part of her brain, Trish could hear Nita trying to talk, could see her friend's frightened face, could see the tall figure, statuelike, as he hesitated not five feet away.

"Nita—*run!*" Trish cried.

"Hey—don't run—everything's cool here." He came a step closer, and Trish stared at his jeans and combat boots, the denim jacket with no sleeves.

"Wyatt," she murmured, and Nita jerked the flashlight beam directly onto his face.

"Hey, you, *put* up your hands!" Nita shouted, trying to control the trembling in her voice.

"And what are you, the vice squad?" Wyatt retorted.

"I mean it—up high where we can see them!" Nita pointed the flashlight like a gun, and Trish stared at her in dismay.

"Nita, what are you *doing?* And what are *you* doing out here by my car?" Trish took a step toward Wyatt as he tried to keep one arm in the air and shield his eyes with the other one.

"Look—you wanna call off Nancy Drew here—"

"Nita"—Trish grabbed the flashlight away—"will you stop playing with that thing? Now"—she turned back to Wyatt—"tell me what you're doing to my car!"

"*Your* car?" And Wyatt turned and looked calmly back at the Mustang. "Your car, huh?" He was silent a moment. He stared at the ground, then he lowered his arms and crossed them casually over his chest. He gazed back at Trish. "I thought this was *my* car. Same make. Same color."

"He must think we're both complete idiots," Nita muttered to Trish.

"Nooo . . ." Wyatt said slowly. "Not both of you."

"Where *is* your car?" Trish demanded.

He thrust his hands into the pockets of his jeans and hunched his shoulders as a cold wind blew through the parking lot.

"I guess someone stole it."

"You guess . . ." Trish eyed him warily. Her heart had begun to beat normally again, and she took a deep breath. "Why would you think that?"

"Why *wouldn't* I think that?" He waved his arms vaguely at the empty parking spaces around them. "I left it around here somewhere. Do *you* see it?"

"Well . . . no . . ."

"So someone must have taken it."

"We don't believe you," Nita spoke up. "We think you're lying."

Wyatt didn't look bothered in the least. He

shrugged his shoulders as if he couldn't help what they chose to think.

"Maybe you just forgot where you parked it," Trish suggested hesitantly. "Maybe it's on the other side of the mall. Maybe you came out the wrong exit."

"Yeah," Nita echoed. "Why don't you just go report it to the security guards or something?"

"And what are they going to do about it?" Wyatt retorted. "Organize a nationwide manhunt?"

Trish didn't know what to do. Part of her was still unnerved and suspicious; part of her wanted to believe Wyatt and sympathize with his plight. She remembered the phone call in the parking lot and shuddered.

"Come on, Nita," she said, nudging her friend's arm. "Let's go."

Wyatt stood there and watched them. Trish moved toward her Mustang, then stopped.

"Would you mind . . ." she asked quietly, "getting . . . standing . . . away from my car?"

"No problem." He held his hands up again and moved backward. "And no weapon either, as you can see."

They got into the car. Trish looked at Nita, and Nita looked out the window at Wyatt. He had turned his back and was making his way unevenly off into the darkness. Both girls looked at each other.

"Oh, Trish." Nita pointed. "He's *limping!* Did I do that to him with my chair?"

"Probably. You hit the poor guy pretty hard."

"Well, where's he going now? To look for his car, do you think?"

"It does happen," Trish mumbled. "Going to the wrong car, I mean. I've done that myself. It's so embarrassing."

"I did it once. Two kids were making out in the backseat, and they got really mad at me."

"Nita, we can't just leave him here. Oh, I don't know what to do!"

"We shouldn't do anything. First off, he was rude to me, and then he scared us out of our minds. And anyway, he might really *have* been trying to break into your car—he could have just made up that story so we wouldn't turn him in to the cops or something!'

Trish started the car, then started following Wyatt.

"Maybe we should just leave." She nodded, trying to convince herself. "Maybe we should just teach him a lesson for scaring us so bad."

"It is awful cold out here," Nita sighed. She waited while Trish pulled up alongside Wyatt, then rolled down her window. "Hey, you," she said, "how're you getting home?"

"Slowly." Wyatt hardly bothered to glance at her. "With bruises and a broken foot."

"I didn't break your foot!" Nita drew herself up indignantly. "And I told you—it was an accident!"

"I can give you a lift," Trish said reluctantly. "Where do you need to go?"

If Wyatt was surprised at their change of heart, he didn't show it. "Wherever you're going—you can just let me out there."

"Well . . ." Trish exchanged looks with Nita. "We were going to get something to eat. Do you want to come along?"

"I'll get out wherever you eat. It'll be fine."

"But where do you live? Don't you want me to take you home?"

Wyatt stopped. He leaned down and peered at them through Nita's window.

"I'm not going home," he said. "I'm not going home right now. Wherever you stop—it's okay."

"I'll ride in back," Nita said quickly, jumping out and climbing in again before he could protest. "There's more room for your legs up there in the front."

"Fine," Wyatt said calmly as he got in beside Trish. "Then you can *attack* me if I try anything funny."

"Some guys like to be attacked for no reason at all," Nita said sweetly.

"So how about the All Night Deli?" Trish broke in quickly. "Over on Crestwood?"

Wyatt leaned back in his seat and closed his eyes. "Cool."

They rode in silence for several miles, then Wyatt shifted, frowning down at the floor.

"Hey, I'm stepping on something down here."

"Oh, those're just tapes. You can put them in the glove box if they're in your way." Trish leaned over and opened the compartment in the dash. "Unless there's something you want to listen to, Nita?"

"I wouldn't dream of it," Nita said. "I'd much rather listen to our passenger's conversation. He's so . . . stimulating."

Wyatt stared out the window. "You'd be surprised."

"Probably not."

Trish made a face at Nita in the rearview mirror and turned into the deli's parking lot. They got out of the car and Wyatt stood for a moment, as if looking around for a pay phone.

"Look," Trish said suddenly. "If you're hungry or something, you could eat with us, if you like."

Wyatt stared at her. "I don't have any money."

"We don't either." Nita looked surprised. "We use charge cards."

"My wallet," Wyatt explained. "It was in my car."

"You keep your wallet in your car?" Nita stared at him, then glanced at Trish.

"I left it there. By mistake."

"Then let me treat." Nita smiled charmingly. "It's the least I can do to make up for the accident today."

"I don't take handouts," Wyatt said.

"Oh, don't be silly," Nita gave him a coy sidelong glance. "I'm sure we can think of *some* way for you to . . . pay me back."

An equally sly smile played at the corners of Wyatt's mouth. "No thanks."

"You can pay me back later," Trish said quickly, herding Nita through the front door. "Let's just go in—I'm starving."

The restaurant wasn't very busy, and they found a booth with no trouble, Nita and Trish sharing a side. Trish scanned her menu, then glanced across at Wyatt. His menu was up close to his face, but he was peering over the top of it, his eyes darting quickly around the room.

"Have you . . . been here before?" she asked politely.

His eyes slid back to her face, making her vaguely uncomfortable. She hadn't really gotten a good look at them earlier in The Eatery, but now she could see how narrow and dark they were, his brows resting low across them. Wyatt looked as though he never missed much of anything.

Now he nodded. "A few times."

"Have you worked at any of the other restaurants around town?" Nita spoke up.

He stared at her with that curiously blank look of his—calm and totally unreadable. Nita tried again.

"I just wondered if you'd worked at any of the other eating places besides the mall."

"Oh. That. Well . . . ." He seemed to be thinking. "I don't just bus tables."

"No?" Nita leaned forward, interested. "You go to school? You have another job somewhere?"

Again his eyes darted quickly around the room. Trish had the sudden impression that he was committing the whole deli to memory.

"I do maintenance work." Wyatt shrugged. "Around the mall. I've just been . . . you know . . . filling in for someone."

"What kind of maintenance work do you do?" Trish asked politely.

"Oh, you know." Wyatt's eyes flicked to the front door—to the front counter—toward the rear of the room where part of the kitchen was visible through a pass-through window. "General things. Repairs. Upkeep. Letting people into places when they forget their keys."

"Oh!" Nita raised an eyebrow. "You pick locks?"

"I can." Wyatt glanced at her quickly, then his eyes slid away. "When I need to."

The waitress brought their food, and for several minutes all of them concentrated on eating. Finally Nita nudged Trish in the side and laughed.

"Just think what fun we could have if *we* could pick locks! We could come to the mall after hours and do all that shopping!"

Wyatt picked up his hamburger, studying it with narrowed eyes. "You wouldn't like being there after hours."

"I don't know," Trish joked. "You're talking to two professional shoppers here. We're pretty dedicated."

She waited for him to answer, but he was staring out the window, his jaw set in a tight line. "Wyatt?" she said gently.

His head came around, his eyes sliding from the outside view back to her face. He lifted his right hand . . . touched the fogged glass . . . made small, slow circles with his fingers. Trish could see his dirty fingernails, and the way they'd been bitten down to the quick.

"The mall's different then." His voice hesitated, lowered. "You wouldn't like it," he said again quickly. "It's not what you think."

"What do you mean? It's just a bunch of stores and food places." Nita laughed, but she sounded unsure. "It's just a place to have fun."

"Fun?" He was silent for a long moment. "It *can* be fun. But nobody *really* knows that mall. Not really." Again his voice drifted off, sank to a whisper. "It has . . . life. You know? Like . . . thoughts. Like . . . a weird kind of . . . mind."

A long, uneasy silence settled down. Nita turned her attention back to her coleslaw. Trish sat there staring at her plate, her appetite suddenly gone.

"Well," Nita announced at last, and Trish looked up in relief. "I've got to get home. I've still got an English paper to write tonight."

"Tonight?" Trish shook her head sympathetically. "You won't get any sleep at all."

"I know. So what else is new? I wish I had someone to keep me company."

Wyatt finished wiping his mouth and tossed his napkin carelessly across his plate. He stared over at Trish.

"So where do you live?" he asked casually.

"Me?" Trish glanced up at him, caught offguard. She tossed a quick look at Nita and said, "Or did you mean both of us?"

"Not too far from here," Nita spoke up. "Why?"

Wyatt shrugged. "I just wondered."

"Is there someplace else you'd like me to drop you off?" Trish asked, sliding out after Nita, slipping into her coat.

"Don't forget, I have to go pick up my car," Nita reminded her.

"Where's your car?" Wyatt asked.

"Back at the mall," Trish said. "But what about you?"

"Well . . ." He ran one hand back through his hair and glanced once more around the room. "I was just thinking then . . . since you're going back that way . . . how about . . . Mayfair. The drugstore on May-fair."

"Mayfair?" Trish sounded puzzled. "But that's right behind the mall, isn't it?"

"Yeah." He thrust his hands into the pockets of his jeans and nodded slowly, as if trying to sort out explanations in his mind. "But . . . I just now remembered I have to pick up some things before I go home tonight."

"So you actually *live* on Mayfair?"

"Well . . . not really. A buddy of mine does. Around there. He can take me home."

"Then you didn't really need a ride. You could have walked to your friend's house," Nita said accusingly.

"No. He works nights. He wouldn't have been there."

"Well, do you think he'll be there now?" Trish asked worriedly.

"He should be. He's supposed to be."

Still puzzled, Trish drove straight to Mayfair. As she pulled up outside the drugstore, Wyatt got out on her side and closed the door.

"So . . . you're going back to the mall now?" He leaned over, peering in at them through her window.

Trish nodded. She took her foot off the brake and eased the car forward. "I hope you find your car. See you later."

"Yeah." He stepped back onto the curb, but Trish could still see his eyes, dark and narrowed, watching them. He reached out and ran one hand slowly, slowly, over Trish's side of the Mustang. "You can count on it."

7

He's weird." Nita glared at Trish as they went slowly through the mall parking lot. "The more I'm around him, the weirder he gets."

Trish shook her head. "That's only because he hasn't fallen under your spell. Any guy who doesn't fall head over heels in love with you, *you* think is weird."

"I know," Nita sighed. "So what do you think—did I make any progress?" She looked hopeful, but Trish shook her head.

"Not one bit. I think this one's invincible."

"Hmmm." Nita frowned. "What am I doing wrong? I must be losing my touch." She leaned her head back against the seat and groaned. "Why do I *care* anyway? I don't even think he's *cute!*"

"Oh, sure you do. *I* think he's cute. In a quirky sort of way."

"Quirky?" Nita echoed. "Oh, that's quaint, Trish. Very quaint. Quirky . . ."

"Okay, different then. Intriguing."

"Weird," Nita insisted. "What a crazy night. We almost get mugged, and you invite him to dinner."

She stared at Trish as her friend stopped the car and lowered her head onto the steering wheel. "You're too softhearted," Nita added, reaching over to hug Trish. "You *want* to be suspicious of people—but you just think they're all basically good and they all have honest motives."

"I'm not that naive, Nita. *Someone* out there planned to terrify me today—and they did a pretty good job of it."

"Yeah, well, *remember* that next time you go giving people a ride."

"You were as bad as me! You were the one who kept coming on to him!"

"I know. I'm hopeless." Nita hugged her again and climbed out. "This fog is really *awful*—and I *still* have to pick up Imogene clear on the other side of town."

"Have your folks do it."

"They're not home. Too bad they only make themselves scarce on weeknights—otherwise we could have some *great* three-day parties."

Trish chuckled. "Be careful going home."

"You, too."

Trish waited while Nita got in and started her car, then sat for several more minutes, watching her disappear into the fog. She leaned over and rummaged in the glove box for some tapes, then stuck one in, smiling a little as the first strains of classical music washed over her like a soothing balm. *Imogene . . . she's been switching my tapes again.*

She put the car into gear and started off, heading toward the main exit. To her alarm, the car sputtered and began to jerk, and as she gripped the wheel with both hands, she felt the momentum fading beneath her.

"Oh, no—what now?"

She floored the gas pedal, but the car wouldn't go. With one last shudder, everything seemed to die, and the car coasted slowly to a halt.

Bewildered, Trish pumped the accelerator. Nothing happened. She turned off the heater, the tape deck, and even her headlights, and pumped again.

Nothing.

Her eyes swept over the dashboard, over the needle on the gas gauge.

Half full.

"Dammit," Trish muttered. "What's wrong with this thing?"

Groaning, she beat her forehead gently against the steering wheel, then looked forlornly out her window. The parking lot was a black smoky hole around her, and as she lifted her eyes slowly to the windshield, she could swear that the fog had thickened in just the last two seconds, swirling on and on forever.

"What am I going to do?" She was whispering, angry at herself, yet trying to stay logical. The pay phones in the parking lots were scattered few and far between, and she knew she wasn't close to any of them. The last thing she wanted to do right now was to go wandering around through the fog trying to find one that worked. "Stay calm," she hissed between clenched teeth. "Stay calm . . . calm . . ." She pressed her hands to her face and realized that her whole body felt chilled.

It came to her then that she really had very few

choices—either take a chance walking back to the drugstore in the fog or go back to the mall and try to find a security guard to help her. She imagined what it would be like walking all alone to the drugstore and opted for the mall.

The streetlights weren't much help at all. The fog was so dense that they barely showed through the darkness, and as she began walking, she realized that Nita had taken her flashlight. She walked quickly, her shoes making staccato sounds on the pavement. She'd always hated those sharp, stabbing sounds—in the movies those sounds always meant that you were totally alone, and very frightened, and they echoed around you, and sounded ten times louder than they really were.

For one moment Trish actually tried to pretend she was in a movie, and her frightened footsteps were being made by someone offstage, and she was only on a make-believe set, not in any real danger at all.

But of course I'm not in danger—why should I be in any danger? That phone call today was just a sick joke and it's over with now—completely over with. What am I thinking? This isn't anything too scary—I've been in worse situations. People have car trouble every day—nothing to worry about—I'll just be glad it happened close to the mall where I can get help.

Trish stopped, her heart leaping into her throat.

Was that a scraping sound?

She remembered how Nita had heard something, too, when they'd walked out here together from work tonight—a footstep, she'd thought? *But look around you,* Trish argued to herself. *Look around you—there's no place for anyone to hide.*

Except in the fog. . . .

Trish halted midstride, jamming her hands nerv-

59

ously into her pockets. She strained her eyes through the clammy darkness, searching in vain for cars, people, some sign of life. The theaters had let out hours ago, emptying what few lots had still been occupied, and the pale shimmer of the mall lights in the distance seemed almost like a dream. She knew she was probably just imagining it, but all around her she felt as if the fog were inching in, closing her off a little more. *Like it's trying to keep me here . . . like it's trying to keep me away from the mall. . . .*

Trish began to run. Ducking her chin into her collar, she squinted against the mist and hurried in the direction of the theaters. From far, far off into the night strange noises drifted out to her, raising goosebumps along her arms—*that scraping sound again? . . . the slam of a car door?*—but she refused to stop and look, and only went faster. As the mall entrance came into view at last, she put on a final burst of speed and threw herself against the glass doors.

"Hello! Is anyone there! Can someone let me in!"

There was no answer.

Pressing her face against the glass, she tried to see deep into the shadowy interior, but nothing seemed to be moving. *There has to be someone here . . . there has to be . . .*

Another entrance. There had to be some other entrance where a security guard might be patrolling. Trish felt her heart sink at the thought of running clear around the mall, trying every set of doors, but there didn't seem to be any other choice.

"Damn! Why couldn't this have happened at home!"

She backed away from the doors, not watching where she was going, and felt her foot come down on something hard. As it rolled out from under her, she twisted and fell to the pavement. There was a rip of cloth, and as she tried to stand, a warm gush of blood oozed over one of her knees. Wincing from the pain, she stumbled a few steps, then looked down, spotting the broken bottle she'd tripped over. *Great . . . as if things weren't bad enough already.*

More frustrated than ever, Trish started along the side of the building, keeping close to the wall beneath the sidewalk overhang. As she came to each new entrance, she banged on the doors with her fists and tried to look inside. Every view was the same—wide, dim corridors; floors patterned with thick shadows; empty escalators, their steps frozen in place; uneven tiers of closed shopfronts and deserted counters and darkened window displays.

"Please!" Trish shouted. "Is anyone in there? Can anyone hear me? I need help! *Please!*"

She rattled the bars on the doors and searched desperately for a guard. But the only people who looked back at her were the mannequins, mocking her with painted smiles.

"Please!" Trish cried again. *"Someone!* Please help me!"

Where are those security guards? She wasn't exactly sure just where the security offices were located— wasn't sure which entrance would be closest to any of them.

"Please!" Trish screamed again, trying yet another door. "I need help—will somebody please let me in!"

She stepped away from the doors and continued on around the building, hesitating when she realized where she was. The dingy alleyway ran behind the south wing of shops on the main floor and was cluttered with dumpsters and piles of old litter. Some smaller deliveries were often made here, and a line of doors opened from the backs of the stores onto the narrow lane. *I couldn't be lucky enough for someone to have left one of them unlocked . . . could I?*

And then she saw a light.

For a moment she thought she was imagining it—the soft glow slanting out from the door at the end of the alley. But as Trish held her breath and slowly approached it, she heard the creak of old hinges, saw the door swing outward, and stopped in her tracks as someone came out onto the stoop. For a long moment he stood there, as if listening, and then he propped the door open and disappeared back inside.

"Hello?" Trish ran forward, relieved when the figure reappeared in the doorway. "Hey—can you help me? I work here, and I'm having car trouble."

She stopped again, several feet from the doorway. The figure hadn't moved as she'd come closer, and now, as she peered into the soft light, she could see his security uniform, the brim of his cap low on his forehead, the faint flicker of cigarette ash dangling from one of his hands. He was wearing black gloves, and as Trish continued to stare, he took a step backward and reached slowly towards his belt. Trish automatically held up her hands.

"Really—look—I have an ID! My name is Trish Somerfield and—honest—I'm really having car trouble—"

She could see him more clearly now. He was wearing a pair of dark-tinted glasses that completely hid his eyes, and his face registered no emotion of any kind.

"My car," Trish said again, lowering her hands to her sides. "I don't know what's wrong with it—I can't get it to start."

She saw him nod, and as he took a keyring from his belt loop, his other hand absently pulled the brim of his cap still lower over his forehead. He stood aside and motioned her to come in.

"Oh, I thought nobody was here!" Trish threw him a grateful smile as she passed. "I was really getting scared—I didn't know what I was going to do!"

It was all she could do not to grab the guard and hug him. Now that she was up close, she could see the thick black hair curling wildly out from beneath his cap, and across his right cheek a jagged scar sliced down from his earlobe to his chin. Trish stared at it, morbidly fascinated, then turned her head in embarrassment. She couldn't tell if he'd seen her staring or not.

"Where's your car?" he muttered. He had a strange voice, she thought—a low, guttural sort of growl—and she had to strain to really hear him.

"In Z lot—near the main highway. It was running fine, and then it just quit. I can't believe this happened."

"You should . . . shouldn't be walking out there all by yourself. You should . . . be more careful."

"I know—only this was the closest place—" Trish broke off as the guard turned away.

He walked off several feet, started to turn around, then stopped with his back to her. "You . . . you shouldn't really be here. Not now."

"Well—I just thought I could use your phone. I was so scared—"

"Of course," he said slowly. "Of course I can do that for you. The important thing is that . . . that you came. That you . . . found me."

"Yes, that's how I feel, too."

"Your knee," the guard interrupted. "It's bleeding.

Let's take care of you first. Then we'll worry about . . . about the phone."

Bewildered, Trish looked down at her leg. Her jeans were ripped over her left knee, and there was a large smear of blood clotting across the torn, dirty material.

"I did it when I fell." She touched her knee gingerly, wincing again at the pain. "I tripped on a broken bottle."

"I'll fix it," the guard said. "Come with me."

He moved off into the shadows, and Trish watched him, noticing for the first time the general clutter around her. They seemed to be in some kind of storeroom, and there were stacks of boxes and crates, several huge garbage cans, and shelves and shelves of food supplies.

"Where are we going?" she asked.

"There's a first-aid kit right over there in that closet. Don't worry. You're . . . safe now."

Trish couldn't resist another look outside as he reached over and closed the door. "I don't think I can go back out there by myself," she said, and saw the guard nod his head.

"Of course you can't. And I wouldn't let you."

"I just need to call someone to come and get me. I can always come back for my car tomorrow."

Disappearing for a second behind a stack of boxes, he mumbled something, and she moved toward the sound of his voice.

"I'm sorry—what did you say?"

"I said . . . that'd be the smart thing to do." He made a sound deep in his throat that might have been a laugh. "You'll have to excuse me—I've been sick. . . . A terrible cold—bronchitis, actually."

"Oh, I'm sorry." Trish smiled. "I guess that's why I haven't seen you around here."

His shoulders stiffened. "What do you mean?"

"Just that I don't recognize you. But then I only started work here a few days ago. Not everyone who works here looks familiar to me yet."

"I work nights," he said quickly. "But then . . . as I said . . . I've been sick."

"It must be strange working here at night." Trish watched as he opened a door, reached inside, rummaged slowly around on some shelves. "Are there a lot of guards here at night?"

"No. No . . . just me."

"Well, don't you ever get scared being all alone here? Isn't it kind of creepy?"

"No," he said again, so suddenly that she glanced at him in surprise. "I mean . . . no . . . it doesn't scare me. I like it. It's much nicer when . . . when there's nobody here."

"You probably get a lot of thinking done, right?"

"Yes," he said. "Dreaming of . . . of things you really want most."

"You do that?" She smiled.

He was silent a moment, then his voice seemed to soften. "Yes."

"I do, too. Like a decent grade on my book report tomorrow." She laughed and added, "And to get along better with my manager."

"She's . . . she's not very nice to you." It was a statement, not a question, and Trish glanced at him again, surprised.

"No, she's not, really. We don't get along at all. I don't know why."

"She makes you unhappy."

"Sometimes. Actually, yes." Thinking of it now, Trish sighed. "See, the thing is, I really love my job. I work at Muffin-Mania, and it's really fun. What I hate is going in there every day and wondering if Bethany is going to start in on me about something." She sighed again and gave him an apologetic smile. "I don't know why I'm telling you all this. It really doesn't have anything to do with you."

She could see his stony profile, and the corners of his mouth seemed to move slowly in a secret sort of smile.

"Come over here," he said.

She moved forward, seeing the small white box in his hands.

"Oh, please don't bother about my leg—it's not even hardly bleeding anymore. If I could just use a phone—"

"You don't want it to get . . . infected," he said. He motioned her to come closer, and she took another step forward. "I won't hurt you."

Smiling a little, Trish came up beside him. "I wasn't worried about that. I just don't want you to go to the trouble. And I really need to get home."

"Yes." He nodded. "After I fix your leg."

Puzzled, Trish watched as he turned his back to her. She heard the soft liquidy sound of something being poured, and then he was facing her once more, holding out a large piece of gauze.

"This will only take a minute," he said softly. "Turn this way. I promise . . . you won't feel a thing."

As she nodded and moved closer to him, her arm accidentally knocked against an open crate, dislodging it, spilling its contents all over the floor. As Trish jumped back in alarm, she watched as bottles broke and shattered across the floor.

"Oh, no—look what I've done now!"

Dropping to her knees, she immediately began

picking up the shattered pieces, gathering them carefully into a pile.

"Leave them," the guard said quietly. "It doesn't matter."

"Oh, I am just so *sorry!* I am such a *klutz!*" Glancing up as she apologized, Trish worked the shards onto a piece of cardboard and then stood up again, looking around the room.

"Your leg," the guard moved toward her, the piece of gauze level with her face. She could smell it from here—a strange, sweet sort of smell. "We can take care of that afterward," he said.

"There—I'll just put these in the trash." Trish went quickly toward the corner, where a huge portable trash can stood on wheels. "Can I pay for the damage? I just feel so awful about this—"

"Come back to me," the guard said quietly. "Come back to me now."

"Yes . . . yes . . . just let me do this first—"

Trish leaned over the trash can, the cardboard and glass held carefully in her hands. The can was already full of litter—bags and bags of it—mounded one on top of the other so that they reached nearly level with the rim.

"I hope no one hurts themselves," Trish mumbled, leaning closer over the can, carefully disposing of the sharp fragments. "You don't think anyone will reach in here and cut themselves, do—"

But the rest of the sentence froze in her throat, and her mouth opened in a wide, silent scream.

The topmost trash bag lay only inches from Trish's face. A long, irregular tear had already begun to separate the dark green plastic, so it was easy to see what was inside.

The girl's face was staring out, eyes dull and glazed with lifeless horror.

Her cheeks were scabbed over with crusted blood.

And like a macabre piece of jewelry, the dark red end of an ice pick protruded from the center of her throat.

8

As Trish stumbled backward, she felt the guard's arms go around her, keeping her from falling.

"What is it?" he said tersely. "What's wrong?"

All she could do was point—point and cover her mouth to keep from being sick. As he pushed her away from the trash can and leaned over to examine her gruesome discovery, Trish fell back against the wall and closed her eyes to keep the room from swaying around her. When she opened them again, she saw the guard's back stiffen, saw his head jerk back at her over his shoulder, saw him straighten up again, and grab the walkie-talkie on his belt.

"Sam." His voice was thick but surprisingly steady. "I need help down here. Gourmet Shop. The stockroom."

"Oh, my God—" Trish whimpered, and he took a step toward her.

"You've got to get out of here," he said calmly.

"Oh, my God—my God—"

"Do you hear me? You have to leave here . . . before the police come."

"Is it—is she—" Trish saw him talking, yet she couldn't hear his words, couldn't understand what was happening until he took hold of her shoulders and started steering her through the boxes to the back door. "What—what are you doing? We've got to call the police—"

"I've already radioed for help. Do you understand? If anyone finds you here, they'll want to question you," he said quietly, hurrying her along. "They'll want to keep you here and ask you lots of questions. I could lose my job. Do you understand what I'm saying? What I did tonight—letting you in like this— is strictly against the rules. I could lose my job and get in all kinds of serious trouble."

"We've got to get help," Trish insisted, pulling at his sleeves, stumbling as he guided her swiftly toward the back. "Who is it? Does she work here? What could have happened—"

"Listen to me. You have to listen. You have to try and understand," he repeated once again. "You've got to get out of here. My job depends on it."

"How—how will I get home—"

"I'll call you a cab. Go outside, and go around the building. Wait by the theaters. Do you hear me? Now, what's your address?"

"My . . . address?" Trish repeated stupidly.

"Where do you live? I need to know. I need to tell the cab company when I call them."

"Oh . . . um . . . two-fifteen Woodfield."

"Will there be someone there?"

"What?"

70

"Your parents," he said patiently. "Will your parents be home?"

"No, she—my Mom's out of town. She won't be back till—till Monday night."

He nodded slowly. "I'll call as soon as you leave, and you wait by the theaters for your ride." Numbly she saw him pry open her hand and press some money into her palm. "Take this, and just go home. No one ever has to know you were here tonight. That will be better for both of us, won't it?"

Trish nodded mechanically. "I'm—I'm so sorry—"

"It will be all right."

"That I came in—that I found—"

"It was an accident," he murmured. "I'll take care of everything."

"What did you say?" Trish felt the cold shock of air as he pushed her outside. She looked helplessly up into his face, but saw only her own pale expression looking back at her from the dark glasses. For a long moment things seemed strangely paralyzed, as if neither of them could move.

Then the door closed, and he disappeared.

A gust of wind whipped Trish's hair around her face, stinging some feeling back into her cheeks—some coherence back into her brain. *It couldn't be . . . a body? Who was that? How could it have happened?*

From some vague corner of her mind came the nagging insistence that she ought to know who it was, that there was something remotely familiar about that poor dead face—something she'd seen before. *But it was so mutilated—how could anyone recognize who it used to be?*

She didn't remember getting back to the theaters.

She didn't remember walking back around the building and she couldn't imagine later how she'd ever found her way so quickly through the fog. As the headlights of the cab came into view, she drew back beneath the overhang and huddled there until the driver leaned out his window and rudely demanded to know if she wanted a ride or not.

Getting home was a complete daze to Trish, images whirling and stabbing through her during the whole drive there. Strange, she thought, what peculiar things managed to stick in your mind in a time of crisis. She could see the end of that ice pick, sticking out of the smeared, bloody flesh, and she could hear the low, calm tone of the guard's voice, and she could feel the pressure of his hands on her arms, on her back as he'd taken her out to the alley. *How can I act like nothing's happened?* she thought miserably. *It'll be all over the news tomorrow, and I'll remember, and how can I act like nothing happened?*

She wished more than anything that her mother were home. She didn't want to be alone in the house. She resisted the urge to pick up the phone and call Nita as soon as she walked in the door—Nita would know at once that something horrible was wrong, and she'd be able to get it out of her. And Nita had never been known for her discretion. Besides that, Nita's parents were probably home now, too, and Trish knew they wouldn't appreciate a frantic phone call at this hour. *This hour. . . .*

To Trish's amazement, it was way after midnight. As she drew every shade in the whole house and checked and rechecked every window and door, she reminded herself again that she couldn't tell *anyone* what had happened. She couldn't take a chance of getting the guard in trouble—not after he'd been so nice to her. He'd put his own job in jeopardy to help her out—he'd even given her cab fare home. Strange . . . she'd never even thought to ask him his name. She'd given him hers, but she'd never heard him mention his name, not even once.

She slept fitfully, her dreams full of terrors and grisly surprises. In one especially vivid nightmare, she didn't notice the trash bag in time, and she plunged her hand inside, touching the dead face, drawing her hand back again with pieces of bloody skin stuck to her fingers. Gasping, Trish bolted up in bed, her nightgown soaked with sweat, her heart pounding. The clock read three; the house was huge and silent. *Oh, Mom, of all the times for you to be out of town. . . .*

She saw the sun come up. She heard the newspaper hit the front porch, and without even bothering to get dressed first, she raced outside and opened it to the front page.

Politics.

Bomb scare.

Blizzard in the northeast.

But no murders.

Nothing about the mall.

Bewildered, Trish went back inside and pored over the paper from front to back. The only mention at all about the mall was the huge sidewalk sale scheduled for that weekend. No mention of bodies or accidents, no mention of foul play—nothing. *Maybe it didn't make the morning edition,* she told herself. *For some strange reason this particular murder just didn't make the morning deadline. But it must have made the morning broadcasts.*

She turned on the radio and listened while she dressed for school. All the usual stories, the sports, the weather.

The mall wasn't news today.

She could hardly concentrate in class. The book reports went by in a blur of garbled discussions she couldn't even hear. Nita kept throwing her questioning looks while Trish stared back blankly, and Imogene even had to remind her to change for last-period volleyball.

"What's the matter with you today?" Nita chided her as she gave Trish a ride to work. "You act like you're under an evil spell or something."

"Have you heard anything about the mall?" Trish gave her a puzzled look. "Anything . . . at all?"

"Well, yeah, the sidewalk sale is this weekend, and it's going to be a nightmare." Nita looked at her strangely. "Why?"

"No reason. I just wondered."

"What happened to your car anyway? How come you needed a ride today?"

"It's . . . it's broken. I mean . . . I don't know what's wrong with it. It broke down on me last night. At the mall."

"You're kidding. You mean right after you dropped me off?"

Trish nodded vacantly. "It's okay—I called a tow truck, and it's at the station now. You can drop me off after work."

"So what did you do?" Nita persisted. "Why didn't you call me?"

"I . . . I called a cab," Trish murmured. "I didn't think you'd be home yet. It was late and—"

"Trish, that was so *dumb!* Anyone could come along and just snatch you off the street like that!" Nita gave her a stern look. "Next time you *call* me—I don't care how late it is. You could have left a message! Someone would have come and gotten you."

"I wish I had," Trish said solemnly. "But really, Nita, didn't you hear anything about the mall today?"

"What's with the mall, anyway? I told you—just the sidewalk sale."

"Yes," Trish murmured. "That's what I meant, the sidewalk sale. I mean . . . I just wanted to make sure it was *this* weekend."

Nita gave her a funny look and jabbed her in the side with an elbow. "Wake up, Trish. Focus in here, girl. You can't take on Bethany in this condition."

And it was strange, Trish thought, trailing along after Nita through the parking lot, through the bustling corridors of the mall, how normal everything looked this afternoon. She'd expected to see police swarming everywhere, crawling through the stores, up and down the alleyways, searching storerooms and trash cans and loading docks and even delivery trucks, standing thick with notebooks in hand, questioning innocent shoppers as they hurried past. *"Excuse me, ma'am, do you know anything about a dead girl in a garbage bag?"* When Nita grabbed her to get her attention, Trish nearly screamed at her.

"What is *wrong* with you?" Nita demanded, patience wearing thin. "You are acting so *weird* today!"

"I'm sorry. I'm just . . . thinking about other things."

"Obviously." Nita shook her head and started up the escalator, leaving Trish to go in the opposite direction downstairs. "Eat a muffin or something. You don't look too good."

Oh, Nita, if you only knew. . . . Trish nodded and began to walk toward The Eatery, weaving in and out of the crowds, keeping her eyes open for the sight of a uniform. She couldn't believe it—not a single policeman anywhere. And then another thought struck her, and she stopped midstride, not even conscious of people glaring and running into her.

She searched until she spotted a security guard near one of the water fountains. Forcing herself to be calm, she walked over to him and excused herself.

"Hi. I work at—at The Eatery." She stopped and took a deep breath, encouraged by his friendly smile. He was older and grandfatherly, and his kindly eyes twinkled as he gave her a nod.

"Can I do something for you, young lady?"

"Well, that's just it. I had some car trouble last night when I was leaving"—*a white lie . . . just a little one.* "And one of the guards helped me."

"Well, I should hope so!" He grinned. "That's what we're here for!"

"So I was just wondering," Trish went on, "if I could thank him. It was really nice of him, and I thought—"

"Well, that's awful nice of you. And just who was this gallant gentleman?"

"I don't know his name. But he was tall—had sort of curly black hair—long—and—"

"That'd be Roger." The guard didn't hesitate. "Roger. Only one I know of who has that funny hairdo."

"Do you know what time he comes on duty?"

"Time? Why, he's here now. As a matter of fact, he's just getting ready to go off. Looks like you caught him just in time."

"But—" Trish started to say more, but the guard started off, motioning her to follow.

"Hey!" he shouted, and she saw a tall figure standing outside the pet store. "Roger! Got a young lady here who wants to see you!"

"Thanks." Trish smiled. "Thanks very much."

"No problem." The guard touched his cap and went on his way, and Trish continued over to where Roger was waiting.

"Hi," she said, and her breath came out in a rush, "Am I ever glad to see you—"

She broke off then, as the tall man looked down at her with a polite smile. He wasn't wearing a cap, and his thick black hair curled out all around his face, but instead of the dark glasses, a pair of clear green eyes looked down at her curiously. For a long moment she gazed up at him, her mind racing furiously. *Something's not right—something's not right at all—*

"Can I do something for you?" Roger asked, and his voice was loud and strong and friendly, with a hearty laugh behind it, and as Trish kept staring, she tried to talk but couldn't.

"Hello?" Roger teased, leaning down a little, leaning down just enough so that she could really see his face, his fair cheeks, smooth, without a hint of a scar.

"I—I wanted—" She was stammering now, but she couldn't help it, and suddenly, more than anything, she wanted to turn right around and run back to the alleyway, to look in the dumpster parked outside the back of the Gourmet Shop. "I—I'm sorry—I thought you were somebody else."

"Too bad for me." Roger grinned, and as he started to turn away, Trish suddenly reached out and grabbed his sleeve.

"You don't work at night?" she burst out. "Here in the mall? The late shift?"

"Late shift?" Roger repeated. "You mean the one that ends at ten thirty?"

"No. No—midnight—*after* midnight—"

"You must have this mall confused with another one," he shook his head apologetically.

"Another one? What do you mean? I'm talking about the guards who stay on duty here all night— Sam—someone named Sam—and—and—that *other* guard—that *other* one—you must know who I mean—the guards who stay here till morning—"

"No." Roger shook his head, his smile slightly amused. "I'm telling you, you must be talking about some *other* shopping center. After ten thirty, this whole place goes on alarm systems. We don't *have* any all-night guards here at the mall."

9

Miss?"

As Roger bent down into her face, Trish took an unsteady step back.

"Hey . . . are you okay?"

"Yes. . . ." Trish murmured. "Yes . . . that is . . . I made a mistake."

"What's that?"

"Wrong person." She shook her head, still backing away from him. "Wrong guard. Wrong mall. Sorry."

Without waiting for him to respond, she turned and hurried away, pushing through the crowds, not stopping until she'd reached the south exit. As she burst outside and raced for the alleyway, she could see four different trucks parked along the narrow enclosure, and the doors of several shops standing open. Delivery people were hurrying in and out of the stockrooms, carrying stacks of cartons, and a few of them glanced curiously at her as she paused and leaned against the wall. *They're all looking at me—how can I do this when they're all looking at me?*

Trish walked away, her stomach churning. *What's going on? I don't understand* ... She could see it again, just as clear as day—the bloody face peering out of the plastic, the ice pick plunged deep in the throat. *I didn't imagine it—I couldn't have imagined it*. ...

She waited and waited. She walked slowly around the parking lot, and then she walked slowly around the entire mall. When she got back to the alley, the delivery trucks were still there, so she walked around again. Each time the horrible scene replayed in her mind, she fought down a fresh wave of nausea and forced herself to walk some more. *I have to do this* ... *I have to*. ...

When she reached the alley for the third time, the doors were all closed and the trucks were gone. For a long time she just stood there, staring at the dumpsters lined up along the drive, watching the back of the Gourmet Shop. Finally, in a kind of stupor, she walked over to one of the receptacles and lifted the lid and peered down into the smelly bin.

The dumpster was empty.

Methodically she went down the line, lifting each lid, examining each interior.

All the trash had been picked up. There wasn't a trash bag to be seen.

Half relieved, half horrified, Trish let the last lid fall shut, then screamed as a hand came down on her shoulder.

"What the hell are you doing here?" Storm Reynolds looked down at her in total dismay. "Hunting for bargains?"

"I—my—" Trish sputtered. "My—my friend Nita."

The corners of his mouth twitched. "You're looking for your friend Nita. She's hiding from you in one of the dumpsters."

"No." Trish backed away, still babbling. "She—she lost something—out here—yesterday. She thought—she thought maybe someone—someone threw it away."

Storm folded his arms across his chest and stared at her. "I see," he said slowly. "And just what was it that she lost?"

"Her—her gloves."

"Gloves."

"Good ones. Expensive gloves."

"Ah." He nodded. "And knowing the logic of most people, whoever *found* these expensive gloves probably threw them away rather than kept them."

"Well . . ." Trish spread her arms in a helpless gesture. "I really don't know. That's why I told her I'd look for them."

"Instead of selling muffins." A grin played at the corners of his lips, and he reached out for her. "Come on. If I had to make a guess, I'd say your friend Nita's gloves are keeping someone else's hands warm today."

Trish allowed him to take her arm and steer her back into the mall.

"What are you doing out here?" she asked.

"Me?" He grinned. "Getting some air. You know."

"This is an awful long way for you to come just to get some air. It's clear across the mall."

"Well, would you believe me if I said a little bird told me some cute girl was digging around in the trash cans, and I couldn't resist finding out who it was?"

Trish looked at him suspiciously. "What little bird?"

"Come on." Storm shook her arm and chuckled. "I happened to be getting some stuff in the Gourmet Shop when one of the girls came out of the stockroom and said someone was out there scavenging. Someone —meaning you."

"You mean people saw me?"

Storm tried to look solemn. "It's all over the mall now. Your reputation's shot."

"And so's my job, by the look of things," Trish mumbled as they entered The Eatery and she saw Bethany fuming behind the counter.

"She can't kill you," Storm said smoothly. "There're too many witnesses."

At the mention of the word, Trish went pale, and he stopped and gave her a puzzled look.

"Did I say something wrong? I was just kidding—I didn't mean to—"

"No, it's okay. I have to go now."

Trish went straight to the back, put her things away, and got into her apron. She didn't say a word when she came out to the counter, and she didn't look at Bethany. Five minutes went by without mishap, but as she turned to reach for a new supply of sacks, one of the bakers chose that precise moment to walk by with a fresh tray of muffins, and the two of them collided. To Trish's horror, the tray clattered onto the floor, and muffins flew everywhere.

"That's coming out of your paycheck," Bethany snapped, hovering over Trish as she knelt to retrieve the damage. "Being late to work—being careless—I promise you, that's *all* being written up!"

"It was an accident," Trish mumbled, close to tears. "I didn't see—"

"And antagonizing management," Bethany broke in. "And let's not forget being rude to customers!"

"I have never been rude to customers!" Trish protested hotly, standing up and confronting her. "I have never once been rude to a—"

Her words died in her throat. Standing at the counter was a tall figure with flowing gray hair . . . a gray beard . . . sunglasses. . . .

"If *I* say you've been rude, then you obviously have an attitude problem." Bethany was seething.

"I—I—" Trish stammered, but Bethany grabbed her and gave her a shove.

"Now clean that up. And don't you ever embarrass me in front of the employees again!"

The man was gone.

As Trish stared at the counter, she could see a line of stunned customers gazing back, and in her embarrassment they seemed to stretch all the way to the very far end of The Eatery. She busied herself sorting muffins into the bins, trying to collect herself, trying not to cry. As tears helplessly filled her eyes, she looked across The Eatery and noticed Storm just slipping into the back room of Pizza Park, his face set and grim. She turned her head and saw Wyatt coming out of a utility closet, holding a broom and dustpan. He kept his eyes averted, but he looked angry.

Whirling around, Trish ran to the back and out the side door, racing for the nearest bathroom. Once inside a stall, she locked the door and burst into tears, crying and crying until there were no tears left to cry, her thoughts tumbling out of control through her brain. *He was there again—it was him—the muffin man—standing right there—watching me. How long had he been there—waiting till I showed up—waiting to make another sick phone call? How could Bethany have done this to me! I hate her! I hate her so much! How could she have humiliated me in front of everyone like that—the whole food area—it might as well have been the whole mall! And where did that body go? I know it was real—I saw it myself—I almost touched it last night. And that guard—he looked like Roger only he wasn't Roger—some guy who shouldn't even have been there and I was alone with him—and now he's disappeared right along with that body. . . .*

At long last Trish opened the door and came out. She turned on the water full blast and splashed it over her face—again and again—until her heart began to settle back into her chest and her breathing was normal once more. *What am I going to do?* She leaned forward over the sink and stared at herself in the mirror, feeling horribly sick, yet strangely detached. *I can't tell anyone. I wasn't supposed to be here last night—they might say I sneaked into the mall—they'll arrest me for breaking and entering. They'll think I'm crazy—or worse—that I'm making everything up—a guard that doesn't exist—a body that doesn't exist. . . .*

Getting hold of herself, Trish pulled some paper towels from the dispenser and pressed them tightly to her face. *I can't say anything. Not to anyone. So what do I do in the meantime? That guard—whoever he is—is he here today, too? Watching me? Working somewhere in the mall? And wherever he is, is he the one who killed that girl? And did he really get rid of her body—or does he still have it with him?*

For one moment she actually tried to argue herself out of everything—tried to convince herself that she was just having a bad day—that the gray-haired man was really a nice guy, that the phone call in the parking lot had been for some other Trish and it was just a silly coincidence. That whoever she'd been with in the stockroom last night really *was* a guard, that Roger had just made a mistake about the night shift, that the body was only a mannequin and someone had been trying to play a cruel joke on the guard.

Because suddenly it was just too terrifying to consider the other possibility—that she had walked right into a murder and interrupted the killer while he was trying to hide the body.

So now he knows who I am . . . where I work . . . where I live . . . how long I'll be alone—he even knows there's no man at my house, just a mother who's out of town. Oh, how could I have been so stupid! She couldn't stop berating herself, and she ran back into the bathroom stall and got sick. It could only be a matter of time now for him to find her house, to discover where she went to school. Murderers were so good at that sort of thing, weren't they, when there were witnesses to get rid of?

Stop it! She'd drive herself crazy at this rate, going over and over things, trying to make sense of them all. *The thing is, he didn't kill you—you were there alone with him, you found a body, and he tried to get you out of there.*

Trish stood in front of the mirror again, frowning at her reflection. It would have been so easy to get rid of her if he'd had that in mind—she didn't doubt that for a second. So why had he let her go? *Nothing makes sense—absolutely nothing makes sense. I really am losing my mind. I really must be having the very worst kind of nightmare.*

Just to satisfy herself, she gave her arm a hard pinch and then cried out at the pain.

"Trish? Are you okay?"

Sniffling, Trish stared at the mirror and saw Imogene's reflection behind her own.

"Oh. Imogene." She dabbed hastily at her red, swollen eyes. "I didn't hear anyone come in. What are you doing here?"

"I'm on break." Imogene watched her closely, but asked no questions. "I went by to look for you, and they told me you were . . . upset."

Trish nodded unhappily. "Well . . . that's putting it mildly."

"Take a walk with me."

"Sure, why not. I probably don't have a job anymore anyway."

Imogene sighed. "Cheer up, maybe Bethany'll have an accident."

"What?" In spite of herself, Trish couldn't help but laugh. Comments like that always sounded so funny coming out of Imogene's mouth.

"You heard me. She's just not worth crying over. Come on. I have to go to the loading dock to pick up a delivery someone messed up."

Trish gave a shudder. "That place is so creepy. I hate going there."

"Me, too. That's why I want you to go with me." Imogene smiled, not a bit ashamed of her cowardice.

The loading docks were located in the oldest section of the mall. To reach them required traveling a complicated series of underground passages and tunnels that seemed to wind forever but finally came out into the huge warehouses on the west end of the property. Trish had been there only once—on a quick tour her first day of work—and had hoped never to go back. Now, accompanying Imogene, she thought she'd feel better about the place, but it was just as unnerving as it had been before.

"Just remember," Imogene told her, as they took a service elevator down into the basement, "that it's not *this* level that gets you to the docks. You have to get out here and take *another* elevator down several more levels to the tunnel at the bottom."

Even as Imogene explained it, Trish stepped out and regarded the second elevator with narrowed eyes. It was an old freight elevator, and the only time she'd been on it, it had sounded like it was collapsing all around her. She followed Imogene inside and shivered a little as the doors rattled closed.

"I hate this," she mumbled, and Imogene gave a solemn nod.

"I know—me, too. It's like being in a cage. It's like being in the stomach of some awful monster."

"Imogene," Trish groaned, "please—"

"Sorry. I forgot you're having a bad day."

"Bad isn't quite the word I'd use," Trish sighed. "Try . . . impossible. Try . . . hell."

The elevator hit bottom, bounced a few times, gave a long, deep shudder. The girls looked at each other, then Imogene got the door open and they stepped out.

"I wish they'd put new lighting in these stupid halls," Imogene grumbled, as they made their way through the passages. The ceilings were low, crusted over with peeling paint and cobwebs, and the walls were cool and damp, part of the mall's structure that had been built conveniently into the surrounding mountains. They pressed back against the stone to let someone pass, and then continued on, their footsteps echoing in the gloom.

It was a relief to reach the warehouse at last. While Imogene went off with invoice in hand, Trish stood in the middle of the general chaos, relishing the confusion and noise. There was stock piled everywhere— veritable fortresses of cartons and boxes, shelves and shelves of merchandise. At the far end gigantic doorways opened out onto concrete platforms where trucks were backed up to deliver and receive goods. People rushed in every direction, and she was so involved in watching, that she didn't even notice the delivery man behind her until she backed right into him.

"Oh, I'm so sorry!"

She stooped down to help him pick up his boxes, and she was still talking, trying to apologize, not even looking up into his face.

"This just isn't my day—I seem to be running into everything today. I'm really so sorry. Here—let me help—"

"No problem," the man whispered. "No problem at all."

They stood together, and as she glanced up into his face, she felt her heart freeze within her.

He was wearing a khaki uniform and matching cap. His hair was combed straight back behind his ears, and there was a thick mustache on his upper lip.

He was wearing dark glasses.

As Trish stared in cold, creeping terror, his mouth formed a crooked smile. Some of his teeth were black.

"Thanks," he whispered. "Nice running into you."

Before Trish could even answer, the man had disappeared into the crowd, and as she started to follow him, Imogene came up and took her arm.

"Well, at least that didn't take long. Here—could you carry one of these boxes back for me?"

Trish hardly heard her. She stared off into the milling throng of workers, but the delivery man had vanished.

"Trish, I said—what's the matter?"

"I—" Trish turned and gave Imogene a blank stare.

"I—nothing. Sure. Sure I can help you. Give me one of those."

Imogene threw her a quizzical look but didn't ask any more questions. Together the girls left the warehouse and started their slow route back to the elevators, Trish keeping close to Imogene's side. *It couldn't be . . . it couldn't have been him.* She felt numb all over. She wanted to get back upstairs—back to the light.

They reached the freight elevator and Imogene pushed the button, frowning impatiently when she realized the elevator was already in use. Groaning from the weight of the box, she spotted a trash can in the corner and went over to it, resting one end of her box on the can's edge.

"Yuck," Trish heard her say suddenly, and Imogene drew back, her face twisted in disgust. "What is this in here—a rat?"

And Trish couldn't help herself—couldn't stop herself from walking over, from leaning down and looking inside that trash can while her blood went icy cold and her breath froze in her throat.

It wasn't a rat.

It wasn't even an animal, except that it *looked* like one, with its long, gray stringy hair. . . .

"How weird," Imogene chuckled. "What is this, Halloween?"

Yet she didn't understand why Trish backed away from the trash can, why she looked so horrified as Imogene lifted the long gray wig into the air . . . and dangled the fake gray beard from her fingertips.

10

Trish . . . are you okay?" Imogene asked slowly.

Trish stared at her. She could see Imogene's lips moving, but no sound was getting through to Trish's brain—only the images of sunglasses and ice picks and blood, the whispers of high voices, low voices. *"Nice running into you."*

The same person? The gray-haired man . . . the guard . . . the delivery man . . . the same person? Or just a coincidence?

"Trish?" Imogene had hold of her arm, was shaking it gently. "Trish, do you need to sit down?"

The same person—a murderer?—watches me . . . knows my name. "Nice running into you."

He could be anyone. Anyone. Anyone at all.

"Trish," Imogene whispered, her face anxious.

Trish opened her mouth and looked straight into Imogene's eyes.

"I'm okay," she mumbled. "I . . . felt dizzy for a minute . . ."

"Come on." Imogene picked up her box again. "Don't carry that if you're not up to it. We can kick it onto the elevator and get someone to help us upstairs."

"Don't be silly," Trish mumbled again. "I'm fine."

"Um-hmm," Imogene sighed. "I believe it."

They rode to the basement level in silence. As they got on to the main elevator, Trish held the box close to her as if it might protect her from invisible dangers. *He could be anywhere . . . he could be anyone. . . .*

"Imogene," she said at last, as they stepped off the elevator and proceeded through the main level of the mall. "Do you remember last night when you were talking about the mall—about the shoplifting?"

Imogene nodded. "Yes. I remember."

"And you started to talk about one of your theories?"

"But no one wanted to hear it," Imogene added matter-of-factly. "As usual. I remember."

"Well, *I* want to hear it. What were you going to say?"

Imogene paused, giving a loud sigh. "Damn. They started working on all the escalators again. We'll have to take the stairs." She headed in another direction and cast Trish a pensive look. "Only that there's probably nobody who really knows all there is to know about the mall. When you consider how many times it's been renovated and rebuilt through the years—it *was* one of the very first malls, you know—then there are probably all sorts of hidden rooms and passages that new builders never found out about."

"So you think that ties in with the shoplifting?"

"I think it makes perfect sense that there could be a

ring of shoplifters working right here in the mall—
and I mean right here *in* the mall. They could be
working out of hidden tunnels and storerooms. They
steal things, but the reason the alarms never go off is
because they steal things from the *inside*. There are
probably a million secret ways to get into these
individual stores and then transfer the stolen goods
straight to the loading docks. For all we know, there
could be other ways out of this place *besides* the
loading docks. It's a totally inside job." She stopped,
looking pleased with herself.

"It's a good theory," Trish murmured. "These . . .
these . . . secret passages and stuff . . ."

"Just imagine," Imogene went on, shifting the box
in her arms, glancing seriously over at Trish as they
walked side by side. "They could crawl around
through the ductwork. Elevator shafts. Tunnels.
Crawlspaces. The more I consider it, the more endless
the possibilities seem."

Trish closed her eyes, a slow shiver going from her
toes all the way up to her head.

"I . . . I don't think I'd like to consider those possibilities."

"And then, of course, they'd never be discovered,"
Imogene went on. "They'd be so clever, of course,
knowing all these secret routes. No one could ever find
them. They could just steal things forever and ever."
Her eyes shone behind her glasses. "Quite a perfect
plan, wouldn't you say? You can't deny the sheer
genius of it."

"No." Trish shook her head. "No, I can't deny
that."

"So that's my theory," Imogene said emphatically.
"And here we are at the bookstore. And you still look
very pale to me, Trish. I think you should go home."

"Maybe you're right. Except I have to go back to The Eatery and get my purse."

"And face the bitch," Imogene said thoughtfully. "Just face her, Trish. Don't let her beat you down. I have a theory—"

"Go ahead," Trish laughed tiredly, and Imogene smiled.

"This is only speculation, you understand. I've only picked up hearsay around the mall." She took a deep breath and plunged on. "I hear Bethany's the most frustrated manager on earth—*and* the biggest failure. Rumor has it she's worked at practically every store in the whole mall and failed miserably at every one of them. No people skills. Total lack of communication. Really . . . such a waste. She's just not worth your having a nervous breakdown over."

"I'll try to remember that the next time she mortifies me in front of the whole universe." Trish managed a smile. "Thanks, Imogene."

"Of course." Imogene motioned Trish to stack her box on top of the other, then went into the bookstore. Trish stood there a long moment, sighed, then turned to go back to work.

What am I doing? she thought miserably. *I can't go back there. I can't face all those people—all the other employees in the whole Eatery, all the customers who heard.* She remembered how Storm had looked going into the back room of Pizza Park. She wondered if he'd been there the whole time or what part of the drama he'd actually come in on. Even Wyatt seemed to have arrived just in time to witness her humiliation. *I should have sold tickets.*

Yet there was no avoiding it. She still had to pick up her purse and her coat, and she couldn't leave because she didn't have a car. *Maybe Nita will get my things for*

*me. That's what I'll do. I won't even give notice. I'll just
not go back there and Nita can pick up my things when
we go home tonight—or maybe she can take a break
and get my things for me right now, and then I'll have
some money to get something to drink.*

Having made up her mind, Trish went straight into
the boutique, relieved when she heard Nita talking
from the stockroom in back. As she poked her head in
the door, Nita looked up with a cheery grin.

"Hey! Is it time to go home yet?"

"I wish," Trish grumbled.

"Welcome to retail hell. These aren't customers in
here—these are animals in clothes. Will you look at
this mess? So far I've had three displays knocked over,
a woman who *insisted* I refund her money for a dress
that *she* spilled ketchup on, and—"

"Nita, I'm quitting my job."

"You're what?"

"It's a long story," Trish sighed. "I just don't want
to go back there right now. Can you get my things for
me?"

"What happened? Did Bethany go off the deep
end?"

"I really don't feel like explaining now, okay? Will
you do it?"

Nita shrugged apologetically. "I can't right this
minute. But as soon as the dressing rooms empty a
little . . ." She gave Trish a quick hug. "Since Freida
bailed out on us, we're shorthanded now. I keep
hinting to Pat that you'd be perfect for the job—"

"Nita, I don't want anything to do with this mall,"
Trish said quickly. "I just want to get out of here."

"What's wrong now?" Nita began, but a customer
came up just then with a question. "I have to run—
where will you be?"

"I don't know. Around. And Nita—" Trish looked at her imploringly. "Later—when you have some time—I really have to talk to you."

Nita's glance was half anxious, half amused. "More phone calls?"

"Not exactly. But it's . . . serious."

Nita's look changed to puzzlement, and she nodded. "I'll find you, then." She started past Trish, hesitated, then whirled back around, grabbing her friend's sleeve. "Oh, I almost forgot—it's the most horrible thing!"

Trish eyed her suspiciously. "What?"

"That dress," Nita moaned. "That beautiful white dress that was so *you*—"

"What about it?"

"Gone."

"What do you mean, 'gone'?"

"I mean gone. Stolen. Disappeared. Just like that. It was here last night when we left, and when Pat was working this morning someone came in to put it on layaway, and it was gone."

"So you think it was . . ."

"Honestly, Trish," Nita fumed, "how could someone get out of the store with that dress? They *couldn't* have worn it out under a coat! It wasn't something you could just wad up and put inside a purse, for crying out loud. That was a lot of dress!"

"A shopping bag," Trish suggested. "Some kind of tote bag."

"It would have beeped at the door," Nita reminded her. "All our clothes are coded to do that. No." She shook her head, bewildered. "It's a mystery to me. And such a shame. Like I said, that dress was made for you and *only* you!"

Trish nodded and left the store, Imogene's theories

clicking off in her head. *Secret passages . . . tunnels
. . . ductwork. . . .* It really wasn't that farfetched, she
concluded—Imogene just might have something
there.

But at the moment there were other things more
troubling to Trish than a stolen dress, and she walked
slowly, trying to sort them out in her head. *The man
at the counter . . . the wig in the trash can . . . the
guard . . . the body. . . .* She couldn't actually believe
now that that phone call in the parking lot had only
been a coincidence, meant for some other girl with her
name. Once before the calculating cleverness of everything had chilled her—and now she felt even more
fearful of what was happening. She felt more than ever
that she should tell someone, and yet again it struck
her how incredible it all sounded—that she had
absolutely no proof, that things were all confused and
mixed up. How could she go to the police with nothing
that made any sense? They'd be just like that smug
security guard she'd gone to for help after the phone
call yesterday—they'd patronize her and laugh and
call it some crazy teenage prank. She didn't know
what was worse, feeling so alone *not* telling anyone or
feeling even *more* alone *trying* to tell someone.

She decided to windowshop to pass the time. She
still wasn't quite ready to face Bethany or The Eatery
or anyone else she knew down there. The memory of
the whole incident still made her cheeks flame in
anger and embarrassment. She went up to the third
level of the mall and contented herself strolling slowly
along the walkways, stopping to examine the window
displays, reading every sign. It was mindless work,
and she didn't have to think about anything, and after
a while she began to feel calmer. *Children's clothing
. . . sportswear . . . toy store . . . computerware. Furni-*

ture . . . golf shop . . . health food . . . office supplies.
She walked slowly, staring at the people, slightly
mesmerized by the colors, wondering idly what she
would buy if she had the money. *It's because I'm so
unhappy and confused about everything—it's because
I'm so mixed up. The delivery man in the warehouse
was a real delivery man. He'd never seen me before—
he was just teasing. He didn't have anything to do with
the guard or that wig or . . .*

*I have to stop this. I have to stop this right now. If I
don't stop right this very minute, I'm going to be seeing
psychos everywhere—every salesclerk, everyone in any
kind of uniform, every single shopper in this stupid
mall.*

Rounding a corner, Trish saw a vacant store on her
left, obviously in the early messy stages of remodeling.
A makeshift tarpaulin of gray plastic had been thrown
over the doorway to discourage curious onlookers,
and the huge display windows on either side were
empty, their glass streaked with grime and samples of
old paint. Slowing down, Trish stared at the entrance.
She couldn't hear any sounds of hammering or saw-
ing from inside—no voices of workmen. Maybe no
one had even been working here today—maybe the
store had been empty and silent all day long. *What a
perfect place to hide. What a perfect place to watch
from.*

From some remote part of her brain, Trish felt her
feet moving forward. She was just outside the tarpaulin now. All she had to do was to open it and go in. She
could hear shoppers passing behind her on the walkway. *What am I doing? I don't really want to do
this—I don't really want to know what's inside here.
Besides, I can't do it now, everyone can see me.
Someone's bound to stop me.*

Her hand went slowly up to the plastic. She felt the stickiness of it as she started to push it aside.

Without warning the tarpaulin swept open.

As Trish stared in shock, a huge workman stepped out, his hardhat tipped down toward his nose, a pair of goggles fastened loosely over his eyes.

"Well, well." He grinned at her. "What have we here?"

Screaming, Trish turned and ran, shoving people out of her path, trying to lose herself in the crowds. In her mind she could hear him coming after her, heavy boots thudding on the walkway—faster, *faster*—and as she saw the escalator up ahead, she jumped onto it and started running down, totally ignoring the "Out of Order" sign. Halfway to the bottom, she forced herself to look back and then stopped.

No one was behind her. No one had followed her on.

She stood there then, on the motionless treads, her grip loosening on the handrail. She could see people swarming below her, like so many ants, and again she looked toward the top of the escalator, just to satisfy herself one more time that she wasn't being followed.

Breathing a sigh of relief, she shifted her weight and started down to the next step.

There wasn't even a warning.

As the escalator gave a sudden, violent lurch, Trish grabbed out wildly for the railing and touched nothing but air.

11

I didn't see her . . . I swear . . ."

The voice drifted into fuzzy consciousness, and as Trish tried to go toward it, all she felt was a curious mixture of pain and numbness.

"She was just there. I hit the switch by accident— we started the damn thing up—and then we saw her falling—"

Moaning, Trish tried to move again. There was a low rush of sound, growing louder and louder, and as her eyelids struggled open at last, she saw a whole sea of strange faces above her, and the roar was the soft, frightened murmuring from a crowd.

"What—what—" she murmured.

"Stay still," a voice ordered quietly just beside her. "Stay still and try not to move."

She wanted to see who was talking to her, wanted to grab onto something safe and solid, wanted to scream, to cry, to run far away—but the pain was so bad and she was so confused. She shut her eyes and prayed that when she woke up, it would all be just a horrible nightmare.

"That's it," the voice said again. "That's it. Just stay quiet and don't move. You're gonna be okay."

And there were people in white bending over her, gentle hands going over her body—she wanted to scream—wanted to get away from them. She was so *terrified*.

She forced her eyes open again and thought she recognized Storm . . . Wyatt . . . and floating behind them . . . a pair of dark glasses.

Trish tried frantically to scream, but the darkness swept in and covered her.

Where am I?

As Trish fought her way through the strange, soft darkness, her eyes opened at last, and she saw pale green walls and shadows—a strange room she didn't recognize. Starting up in bed with a cry, she immediately grabbed her head and sank back down upon the pillows. She tried to call for her mother, but nothing came out, and as she turned to get out of bed, she saw a call button pinned neatly to her pillow. *I must be in a hospital. What's happened to me?*

In a painful flash, it all came back—the workman stepping out of the abandoned store, her mad dash to escape, her flight down the broken escalator, and her terrifying fall. Her head was pounding now, and as she put up a hand to touch it, she winced with pain. There was a bandage on her chin, and her face felt stiff and sore. She tried to shift positions and realized that her body felt even worse. Pushing the button, she was relieved when a nurse came in almost immediately.

"So you're awake." The nurse seemed pleased. She took Trish's wrist and held it gently. "You had quite a fall, young lady. You banged yourself up pretty darn good."

"Where am I?" Trish mumbled.

"St. Luke's," the nurse replied, and there was a kindness, a smile to her voice. "We're just keeping you overnight to make sure you're really okay."

"What's wrong with my chin?"

"Hmmm . . . no beauty contests for a while. But Doctor Lane is very good with stitches. You'll be fine."

"Stitches . . ."

"You're lucky. You have a lot of other cuts—not so serious—and you're going to be sore for quite a while, but other than that—"

"It wasn't an accident," Trish mumbled, and she could feel the nurse's eyes on her in the darkness.

"What was that, dear?"

Trish's head felt dizzy, spinning. She put her hand to her forehead and shook her head slowly. "Nothing. Where's my mother?"

"You're quite the mysterious one, aren't you?" the nurse teased. "We couldn't find anyone who'd claim you. Just two practically hysterical friends."

"Nita . . . Imogene . . ."

"Don't worry, they're home now, but we had to put up an awful fight to get them to leave. And what do you know—it turns out you're not really an orphan after all."

"My mom . . . she's out of town. She's in Europe."

"So we found out." There was sympathy in her voice, and Trish tried not to give in to it. "In the meantime, your friends' mother is going to be responsible for you."

"Mrs. Hanson." Trish breathed a sigh of relief. "So I can go home tomorrow?"

"We'll just wait and see what the good doctor says." The nurse laid a cool hand upon her cheek. "I wouldn't be a bit surprised, though."

"Thank you," Trish mumbled. "Thanks for all you've done."

"Ssh . . . get some sleep now. You'll feel better in the morning."

"Thank . . . you. . . ." Trish felt like she was falling down a deep, dark well. She wanted so badly to hold on to the nurse, to her reassuring voice, to her strong hands, but something was pulling her down—down —like she'd fallen down the escalator—and she couldn't hold on.

She didn't know how long she slept this time. She only knew that something had awakened her, and as she jerked restlessly in her bed, she called for the nurse but no one answered. In the darkness of her room, she saw shadows near the window, and her eyes tried to follow them, but her mind was out of focus. She tried to sit up, but her body wouldn't do what she wanted. As her eyelids flickered shut, then open, she sensed another movement—this one near the foot of her bed. And as her eyes widened, she saw something—a tall shadowy figure—and she gave a little whimper of terror.

"Don't be afraid." The voice came out of the darkness, a soft whisper, commanding yet gentle.

It was a whisper she'd heard before.

"Oh, God, no—" She gasped and tried to scoot back in the bed, but pain washed over her in a weakening wave.

"You frightened me, you know. You frightened me

so much. I looked up . . . and you were falling. I thought . . . you were dead."

"Who are you?" She was trying so hard not to cry, but tears were filling her eyes, streaming down her cheeks in the darkness. "Why are you doing this to me?"

There was a long moment of silence. When the voice came again, it sounded shocked and upset.

"You—you think *I* did this? That I could *ever* hurt you?"

"Please—please go away—"

"How could I ever do *anything* to hurt you—you're my *life!* Do you understand? My . . ." His voice trailed off. ". . . My . . . life. . . ."

To Trish's horror, the shadow moved closer, swirling around the side of the bed. As in a dream, she felt her hand move toward the call button . . . felt only space upon her pillow.

"It's not there, you see," the voice went on calmly. "I couldn't take a chance on someone coming in here . . . interrupting us. This is *our* time together. *Our* time."

Gasping, Trish pulled her hand back, and the figure seemed to shimmer, caught momentarily between the darkness and a pale slant of moonlight from the window. "I've been here a long time, you know. Watching you. You look so peaceful when you're sleeping . . . your hair spread over the pillow . . . that tiny little pulse at your throat. You're so . . . so very . . . beautiful. . . ."

"I'll scream. I swear I—"

"I've been watching you for a long . . . long time. Not just here. Everywhere." He was quiet a moment, as if thinking. "You don't see me . . . but I see you."

"Where?" she asked fearfully. "Where do you see me?"

Again he paused, and she thought he was going to answer, but then he went on as if he hadn't heard.

"Oh, I know *lots* of things about you, Trish. What makes you happy . . . what makes you sad." He laughed softly. "What makes you afraid . . ."

"Stop it!" she begged him. "Please! Please leave me alone!"

"I know how your eyes look when you laugh. The way your smile makes your whole face light up. And I know . . . the way you smell . . . your perfume . . ."

"Stop it—*please stop it*—"

"The way you feel. You remember, don't you, when you touched me? You were giving me change. Our hands met. And you were warm . . . soft . . ."

"Don't—" she sobbed.

"And that muffin . . . the taste of you still on it . . ."

She opened her mouth then, opened her mouth to scream, but suddenly his hand was there, clamped hard over her lips, and his whisper was loud and harsh, breathing into her ear.

"Don't do that, Trish—don't make any noise. Someone will hear—someone will come. And this is *our* time—I don't want anyone else to share it. If you don't be quiet, I'll have to . . . to make you stop. I won't hurt you . . . I could never hurt you . . . but I'll do something so you won't be able to talk. Do you understand?"

She could feel his powerful strength, his rapid breathing upon her face. Terrified, she managed to nod.

"Promise me," he said quietly. "Promise me you won't try to call anyone."

Again she nodded. His breathing slowed. His grip on her face relaxed.

"I *have* to tell you this, Trish. So you'll see how much I care about you. I have to tell you, so you'll understand how much I love you. Or else . . . how will you ever know?"

His hand pulled away. His shadow slid back into the corner, part of the other shadows already there.

"I like the red sweater you wear sometimes," he said quietly.

Trish squeezed her eyes shut, biting her lip, trying to hold back her cries.

"You had it on the first day you came to work. It has dark blue trim and long sleeves."

He paused, as if looking into memories. She could tell he was smiling.

"And I like the way you comb your hair back into a ponytail sometimes. It's long and thick and soft. But mostly I just like it hanging down your back. Sometimes I imagine . . . I imagine . . . touching it."

"No," she choked. "Please stop—"

"I know how you look in that white dress," he said suddenly. "I know how you look in it . . . and how you look . . . out of it."

Ice coursed through her veins. Again she saw herself in the dressing room the night before, remembered her feeling of being watched. The mirror. . . .

"Get out of here!" She was angry now—angry and horrified. And as she pressed the covers helplessly to her chin, she felt like he could see her—every inch of her—in the dark. "I'll call the police, do you hear me? I'll call the police and I'll tell them all about you—"

"What?" He sounded amused. "What will you tell them about me?"

"That you're hiding in the mall—that it was you

last night. It *was* you, wasn't it—in the stockroom—
with that body—"

"I'm afraid I don't know what you're talking
about," he said smoothly. "Body . . . stockroom . . .
you must be thinking of someone else."

"And the wig in the garbage can—"

He laughed. "What an imagination you have. I
don't think the police would take you too seriously,
now, do you?"

She was crying harder now, watching the shadow
that hovered against the wall, praying he wouldn't
come closer. When he moved away from the corner
and touched the side of her bed, it was all she could do
to keep from shrieking.

"I've waited all my life for you, Trish," he whispered slowly. "All these years . . . all these . . . lonely
. . . years." He took a long, deep breath and moved
closer. "We're destined to be together. And I promise
you—it *will* happen. Soon. But not just yet. Not till
everything is perfect."

"Someone *will* believe me!" She tried to draw away
from him, felt his hand brush over her arm. "And
they'll come after you—"

"Oh, no, they won't," he said calmly. "No one else
has a place in our world, Trish—*no one else*—just you
and me. Soon . . . very soon . . . you'll see that for
yourself. But in the meantime . . ." His shadow
pulled away again . . . hesitated near the window as if
thinking. "If I *do* hear that you've talked about
this—and believe me, I *will* know—then I'll have no
choice . . . but to hurt your friends. Nita, isn't it? And
Imogene?"

Trish felt herself sinking, deeper—deeper—into a
cold pit of terror.

"You can't threaten me," she murmured. "I'll quit my job. I'll never go back to the mall again."

"Imogene works in the bookstore. And Nita sells clothes at The Latest Trend."

Trish stared into the darkness, dazed. His voice was nonchalant, almost bored. He could have been talking about the weather.

"You live on Woodfield. In the big white house with the blue shutters. Your mother is in Europe now . . . so you're alone . . . until Monday night. Nita and Imogene live on Portland Road. When they drive, it's in the family station wagon. Do you want me to tell you the license number?"

"Please—I don't understand." Trish could hardly get the words out. "What do you *want* from me?"

"Your love." There was a brief silence, then: "Your loyalty." His shadow whirled around, a dark ominous outline against the windowglass. "You must not speak to him again, Trish . . . he has no place in our world. I forbid you to see him."

"Who?" She was so dizzy. She tried to focus on his shadow, but he moved again, disappearing into other shadows along the walls. "Who are you talking about?"

"He is *not* what he seems to be," the voice went on, growing even lower, the whisper barely audible now in the heavy, dangerous silence. "Don't trust him. Whatever you do . . . don't . . . *ever* . . . trust him."

"*Who are you?*" Trish murmured again. "For God's sake—"

"You may call me . . . Athan," he replied. "I am your protector. Your guardian . . . your devoted keeper. I'm very, very close to you . . . *especially* when you can't see me."

Without warning she felt his hand on her cheek. Before she could even react, it slid down her neck and then it was gone.

"You're mine, Trish," he whispered. "I'll be coming for you soon."

A sliver of light sliced across the foot of the bed as the door opened just a crack.

And like a melting shadow, the figure oozed out into the hallway and disappeared.

12

She fell as she tried to get out of bed.

Pulling herself across the floor, Trish managed to get the door open and propped herself in the doorway, calling for help. It didn't take long for the nurse to respond, and with a look of shock, she helped Trish back to bed, scolding her gently.

"Why didn't you use the call button? That's what it's there for. You shouldn't have tried to get out of bed by yourself!"

"But it *wasn't* there," Trish tried to tell her, but of course it made no sense. "It wasn't there, and someone was in my room—"

"No one was in your room." The nurse shushed her, tucking her gently back into bed. "I've been out there at the desk all this time. No one's come in or out."

"Someone was *here!*" Trish insisted. "Someone was in my *room*. I saw him go out in the hall—"

"Okay," the nurse said agreeably, handing Trish a

glass of water, coaxing her to take a small sip. "Okay, if you say so. Tell me—what did this person look like?"

"I don't know." Trish shook her head miserably. "He was just a tall sort of shadow—"

"Did he talk to you?"

"Yes."

"And what did he sound like?"

"I don't know. He was whispering—but it was awful!"

"Ssh, it's all right now. You're *safe* here. Sometimes these medications can make us have the strangest dreams—things can seem very real—but they're only nightmares. Look, I'll stay here with you for a while until you get back to sleep. Would that be okay?"

Trish nodded, hating herself for being such a baby. She wished her mother would come home and take care of her. She wished she'd never even heard of the mall. She wished she'd never tried to run down that stupid escalator. She wished—

What's happening? Everything was all jumbled up in her mind, a mass of fears and uncertainties and pain. She wanted to close her eyes and wake up in the morning to find out that everything in these last few days was only a bad dream.

The next thing she knew, she *was* waking up. Sunlight was streaming through the curtains, and the room was bright and calm. Rubbing the sleep from her eyes, she groaned as her body rebelled in a surge of pain. She'd probably be hurting for weeks—she must have bruised every inch of herself when she fell. As she groaned and tried to turn over, the door opened, and Nita's smiling face peeked through.

"Nita! What are you doing here?"

"Making sure you're still among the living," her

friend teased, closing the door softly behind her. "They wouldn't let me in to see you yesterday, and I don't think I'm *really* supposed to be visiting now, but I *had* to see you. What are you trying to do, scare us all out of our minds?"

You don't know scared, Nita, Trish wanted to say, but she managed a wan smile instead.

"I guess there just wasn't enough excitement in my life." She tried to shrug, but caught her breath in pain. "You know what a show-off I am."

"Right." Nita gave her a cautious hug. "You look awful. You have black eyes."

"Both of them?" Trish groaned. "How am I going to face people at school?"

"You're not going to school. At least not today, anyway." Nita drew back and regarded Trish with a critical eye. "Well, I take it back—they're only a *little* black. Anyway, Mom's coming by this morning to spring you—*if* the doctor says you can leave. I think you should take advantage of all this and stay in bed—*and* let Mom wait on you—for at least a month."

"That's so sweet of your mom," Trish sighed. "I can't think of any place I'd rather stay. Did you get my stuff at work?"

"Yes, and really, I don't blame you one bit for not wanting to go back. I was talking to one of the girls you work with and—"

"But I am going back," Trish said suddenly, and Nita stared at her.

"What?"

"I said—I said, I am going back. I decided not to quit after all."

Nita looked doubtful. "After what happened with Bethany? But I thought—"

"Well, I thought about it, too." Trish avoided Nita's eyes and concentrated on smoothing the covers. "And I just decided that . . . that I shouldn't let her run me off like that. I didn't do anything wrong, so if she wants to get rid of me, she'll just have to fire me."

She glanced up at Nita's surprised face and saw her friend break into a smile.

"I'm proud of you, Trish! That's the spirit! And I bet any *one* of those people who work there will back you up—they *all* hate her, you know."

Trish looked back at her, feeling ashamed. *Quit thinking I'm so brave, Nita—if you only knew why I was really doing this.*

"Imogene's going to spread the word at school," Nita went on. "I'm sure you can make up the work once they find out what happened to you. I think Imogene said she's going to tell them it's a miracle you're still alive—which isn't too far from the truth by the looks of you." She reached down and put her hand gently to Trish's forehead. "The workmen were drunk—they'd been drinking on their break, and when they got back, they just started working on the escalator and turned it on without even bothering to look up. They swore they never saw you. I thought you'd like to know."

"So in other words I don't have some crazy psycho killer after me, is that what you mean?" Trish forced a laugh, and Nita shook her head, chuckling.

"Well, here comes that nurse to run me out. Good luck, kid—I'll see you later."

"Thanks, Nita." Trish tried to wave, but only succeeded in groaning.

Trish was relieved when Mrs. Hanson came to pick her up—the thought of staying in the hospital one more night terrified her. She'd always loved Nita's

and Imogene's mom—a real stay-at-home mom—
and it helped ease the pain of her own mother being
far away. Mrs. Hanson tucked her into the extra bed in
Nita's room and then bustled about making her a
special breakfast on a tray, insisting that Trish stay in
bed and rest, at least for today. Trish was glad her
friends weren't around—she was exhausted and worried and needed time to try and sort things out. The
only thing she was really sure about was that her
frightening stranger—Athan—meant business. She
believed him when he said he'd know if she told
anyone anything. She couldn't take that chance.

Sick at heart, Trish spent the rest of the day tossing
in and out of restless sleep, trying to think what to do.
What *could* she do? Going to the police was out of the
question. Warning her friends was equally as dangerous. The idea of some disguised stranger following her
around the mall, alternately whispering endearments
and warnings—the whole thing seemed like a fantasy,
even to her. She could hardly stand to think about
Nita and Imogene going to work tonight—obviously
he was watching them, too. Were they in danger—
even at this moment? If she stayed quiet and kept him
a secret, would he really leave them alone and not hurt
them? And what "him" had Athan been talking
about? *"He is not what he seems to be. . . ."* Someone
at school? Storm? Wyatt? Someone else at work?
*What does that mean? Is he trying to warn me or just
trying to scare me?*

I can't trust anyone . . . not anyone.

By six o'clock Trish felt like she'd go crazy if she had
to stay in bed another second. She was exhausted with
thinking, with worrying, with trying to make sense of
everything. She was relieved when the Hansons had
dinner plans that night—Mrs. Hanson fixed her some

soup and hot bread and brought her another tray before they left.

"Now, we'll be out late, but Nita said she'd try and call you this evening to see how you are." Mrs. Hanson fussed, straightening Trish's covers, plumping up her pillows. "Normally I'd tell you to ignore the phone, but if you don't answer, she'll probably have a panic attack."

"I'll talk to her." Trish smiled. "Have a good time."

She promised them she'd stay in bed and sleep, but as soon as she heard the car back down the driveway, she painstakingly pulled on some clothes and hobbled into the living room.

There was nothing on television that interested her. She found a packet of cocoa mix in the kitchen pantry and put a kettle of water on the stove to boil. She went slowly to the window and peered out through a crack in the curtains. Was he out there—even now—watching the house, knowing where she was? Watching—waiting—to see if she kept her mouth shut? *Maybe he followed me here this morning. Maybe he's been sitting out there somewhere all day long, just waiting for me to leave.*

She jerked the curtains shut and fought back sudden tears. *I'll never be able to go anywhere again . . . do anything . . . without wondering if he's there . . . without being afraid.*

She jumped as the phone rang. Once. Twice.

The telephone was at the other end of the room and she had to dig it out from beneath a pile of fashion magazines. She could picture Nita standing at the counter at work, shifting impatiently from one foot to the other, frowning, muttering under her breath.

She smiled, shaking her head, and picked up the receiver.

"Hi, Nita," she sighed.

For a moment there was silence.

The sound of soft breathing.

"How are you, Trish?" the voice whispered.

Trish recoiled violently, throwing down the phone, slamming backward into the wall, pressing her hands over her ears to blot out the sound of that voice.

"I miss you . . . but we'll be together . . . very soon . . ."

"No!" Trish screamed.

"Sleep well, my darling . . . sleep well."

13

She was terrified to stay in the house.

She was terrified to leave.

Where is he? Calling from the mall? A car? A house right in this neighborhood? How does he know where I am?

Crying, Trish picked up the phone, started to dial, then quickly put it down again. *He'll know if I call someone—he'll hurt Nita and Imogene. Oh, God, what'll I do?*

She thought quickly, slipping into her coat, scarcely even realizing what she was doing. She'd slip out the back—sneak through the yard, shortcut between the houses. She'd run down to the corner to the library. The library would be open now—bright and busy— full of people. He'd never think to look for her there. She'd be safe—she wouldn't be alone.

She left the light on and turned up the television.

The back porch light was already off, so she opened the door just wide enough to squeeze through. The Hansons' backyard was large and overgrown, tangled with shrubbery, closed in with trees. Their garage stood to one side, a storage shed sat at the other end. It would be hard for anyone to see her back here—even the next-door neighbors. Taking a deep breath, she limped across the grass and squeezed through an opening between some leafless hedges and the garage.

There were clouds tonight—thick strands tangled around a sickly yellow moon. As she ducked down between the houses and came out onto the next block, she paused for a moment to watch the street. There were no cars in sight. The sidewalks were deserted. Dead leaves rattled across the pavement, stirred into life by a cold, raw wind.

Trish pulled her collar around her face and lowered her head. She'd thought it'd be easy, that she'd be able to hurry—but she hadn't counted on the pain. Now, as she tried to quicken her pace, every muscle cried out in protest, and the stitches on her chin felt like they were pulling into themselves. She bit her lip and felt tears brimming in her eyes. *I have to go on . . . I can't stay here. . . .*

She went on through the darkness, starting at each new sound, keeping a sharp eye on the street beside her. Once more she cut through some neighbors' lawns and sneaked furtively between houses, praying that no one would mistake her for a prowler. When she finally spotted the library up ahead, she fell through the front door with a grateful sob.

The light and warmth enveloped her at once, making her weak with relief. She stood for a moment surveying the huge front room—the desks and shelves—the people quietly strolling back and forth, their noses buried in books. *He could be here, too, you know . . . he could be.*

The thought hit her like a cold fist. She leaned back against a bookshelf and took a deep breath, forcing herself to be calm. Of course he wouldn't be here, she argued with herself—she'd been so careful—she'd gotten away and he'd never think to come here.

Still, she couldn't help glancing nervously about as she made her way to one of the smaller rooms. She found an unoccupied desk and sat down, keeping her face hidden within the partition walls. She didn't want to get up and find a book—she couldn't have read it even if she'd wanted to. She just wanted to sit here and be with people and not think—*not think!*—about what was destroying her life.

She crossed her arms on the desktop and lowered her head. She closed her eyes and moaned softly.

She heard the footsteps, coming slowly, very near to her.

She heard them stop.

Right beside her chair.

As Trish's eyes flew open, a scream rose in her throat, then locked there, nearly choking her.

"Well, hi," Storm Reynolds said. "Are you following me?"

All Trish could do was stare. Storm looked down at her and smiled, and then, when she didn't answer, he squatted down on his heels and leaned toward her face.

"I said are you following me?" he whispered.

"What . . . what are you doing here?" Trish mumbled.

"The same thing you are, probably. Trying to keep warm."

Trish kept staring. Her mind felt numb. She couldn't think of anything to say. *"He is not what he seems to be. . . ."*

"Are you studying?" She stared down at his empty hands. "You don't have any books with you."

"Excuse me," he said deadpan. "I thought this was a *public* library. I didn't know you owned it."

"I—I'm just surprised to see you, that's all."

"Yeah, same here. I've been worried about you," Storm said seriously. "I heard what happened at the mall." His eyes moved slowly over her face. "I guess it wasn't an exaggeration."

"I fell," Trish said stupidly.

He gave a slow nod. "How are you feeling?"

She shrugged. She still didn't raise her head.

"Should you really be here, do you think? Shouldn't you be home in bed or something? Recuperating?"

"Why aren't you at the mall?" Trish asked bluntly, and noticed how he hesitated a moment before he spoke.

"Hey, isn't it okay if I have a night off once in a while?" He grinned. "Pizza isn't my *whole* life, despite what you might think."

She didn't smile. She turned her head and buried it in her arms.

"Hey," Storm said softly, touching her shoulder. "You're beginning to scare me a little. I think you should go home."

"No. I can't go home."

"Why not?"

"I mean—I don't want to go home."

There was a long silence. "You're not reading. You don't look like you're studying. Let me guess—you're still looking for your friend Nita's gloves."

Trish suddenly had a wild desire to laugh. A quick

flash suddenly went through her mind, and she saw herself digging through the dumpsters like a frantic bag lady, coming up triumphantly with a green garbage bag in one hand and an ice pick in the other. She heard a strange sound and realized that she really *was* laughing, only she could feel hot tears streaming down her face.

"Come on," Storm said quickly, and his arms were beneath her elbows, lifting her firmly from her chair.

"No," Trish cried softly. "No—let me go—I can't—"

But Storm had a tight hold on her now and was steering her firmly though the library, past the checkout desk, out the front doors.

"No." Trish kept shaking her head, trying to push him away, but he was too strong for her, and she hurt—she hurt so badly all over. "You don't understand—I can't go with you. I *don't want* to go with you—"

She felt the night rush past her, and she saw cars and was vaguely aware that they were in a parking lot, and she was being pushed gently into a front seat.

"No," she begged. "Please—*please*—"

But he was in the car with her now, and the motor was starting, and they were driving away, out onto the street—through the neighborhoods, onto the main road.

"Please," Trish sobbed. "I have to go back. I don't want to be with you—"

"Thanks a lot," Storm said, smiling uncertainly. "It's not that I've never been *told* that in my lifetime —but never from a girl who hasn't even gone *out* with me yet."

"You don't understand!"

"Then tell me, Trish—"

"I can't." She put her hands over her face and tried to choke back her tears. "I—I just can't. You're scaring me. *Please* let me out!"

"Let you out? Right here?"

"Yes!"

"If I let you out at all, it'll be at your house, okay?"

"No! Don't take me home!" Trish uncovered her eyes and looked at him miserably. He was staring straight ahead, one hand loosely on the steering wheel, the other draped across the seat behind her.

"Hey," he said softly. "It's okay. If you don't want to go home, then you don't have to."

She felt frantic—trapped. She thought for one moment about jumping out of the car, but then she realized they'd reached the highway and picked up speed. She gulped down her sobs and stared at him.

"Are you kidnapping me?"

To her surprise, he chuckled softly, giving her a sidelong glance.

"Well . . . don't think I haven't thought about it. But I'm too young to spend the rest of my life in prison."

Tired and frustrated, Trish let her head fall back against the seat. She felt his hand drop lightly to her shoulder and settle there.

"You seem to have a pretty big thing against going home right now. And you sure look like you could use a good friend," he said softly.

Trish stared at the windshield—at the thick black sky . . . at the full autumn moon.

"I feel like I could *be* a good friend," Storm said.

"If you were a good friend, you'd have left me in the library," Trish said wearily.

"Well, okay." He shrugged good-naturedly. "I guess you do have enough friends, at that."

"What do you mean?"

"You and your girlfriends. The tight trio."

Trish felt an uneasy shiver go through her. "How do you know about my friends?" she whispered.

"What do you mean, how do I know?" Storm looked surprised. "You three are always together." He reached for the dashboard, turned on the defroster. "You're lucky. I never had two close friends like that. Not even one close friend."

Trish turned her head and looked at him. He stopped for a red light and his face seemed to grow thoughtful.

"My folks moved a lot when I was growing up. There was never time to make any real friends . . . any real attachments. And when I did—well"—he shrugged, giving a light laugh—"it always hurt too much to have to leave them. So I just stopped with the commitments."

"Why did you always have to leave?" Trish couldn't help asking.

"My dad was in the military. My mom—" For a split second his face darkened. "Mom died when I was eight."

"I'm sorry," Trish murmured.

"Me, too." His smile was forced . . . sad. "She was beautiful. I missed her a lot." Again that strange, dark look. "I still do."

He moved his foot from the brake to the accelerator. The car shot forward, and Trish reached unconsciously for the door handle.

"It'd be nice to have a place you'd never have to leave," Storm went on, and Trish thought he sounded almost wistful. "A place where you'd feel . . ." His voice dwindled, and he shot her a startled look. "Wow. Listen to me."

Trish gazed at him for a long moment but said nothing.

"I don't usually go on like this about myself." Storm looked a little embarrassed, and Trish shook her head.

"It's okay."

"You hungry? You feel like something to eat?"

She shook her head again.

For a long time neither of them said anything. Then finally Storm spoke up.

"It's kind of a funny thing. How news travels so fast around the mall. You'd be surprised at what everyone hears. And knows."

Again Trish felt a strange uneasiness go through her. She glanced at him quickly, then out her window.

"That escalator you fell down—it was out of order." Storm kept his eyes straight ahead. His hand lay still upon her shoulder.

"It—it was an accident," Trish mumbled. "It was stupid of me to get on it."

"The thing is," Storm went on, still not looking at her, "I can't figure out why you tried to go on it in the first place. You strike me as being a sensible sort of girl. You must have been in an awful hurry for some reason."

Trish stiffened. She lifted one hand slowly and rubbed at the fogged up glass.

"It was my fault. I fell. That's all."

"You must have noticed the sign . . ."

She nodded. "I told you, it was a stupid thing to do. I just wasn't thinking."

"Or maybe you *didn't* notice the sign. Maybe something upset you. Or scared you." His eyes shifted, lingering on her face. "You should be more careful. People who aren't careful just end up getting hurt."

Trish wrapped her arms around herself and shivered.

"Cold?" Storm asked.

"I—I had a fight with my manager," Trish said quickly. "I was pretty upset yesterday about that."

He nodded. "Yeah, I know. I . . . saw the whole thing."

"You did?"

His glance was smooth and swift. "Sure. I was busy in the back. Take-out orders. Anyway"—his eyes went to the windshield—"she's probably not going to be around much longer."

Trish looked at him sharply. "Why do you say that?"

"Nobody likes her. She bullies people. And she can't manage worth a damn. The only reason she's been at the mall as long as this is 'cause her old man owns half the stores there. He doesn't know what to do with her either. She's totally incompetent."

"How do you know that?"

"I told you," he said quietly. "News travels."

He coaxed the gas pedal to the floor, and the car flew around a wide curve. Trish caught her breath and put a hand to her throat.

"But you *are* going back, aren't you?" Storm asked quietly.

"What—what did you say?"

"To work. You are going back, aren't you?"

"I—" The pain was worse suddenly—in her face, her head—throbbing—*throbbing*—

"Aren't you?"

The car went faster. She felt like she couldn't breathe.

"Yes!" she exclaimed. "Yes—I'm going back!"

"Good," he said. The car slowed . . . sailed . . . coasted like a gentle wave down the next hill. "That's good," Storm said again. "God, I love this car. What power."

They drove on for several more miles. When Trish felt the car begin to slow down again, she stiffened, instantly alert.

"What are you doing?"

"I want to show you something."

"What?" Her voice rose, and he glanced over at her in dismay.

"Take it easy. You're going to like this."

"I want to go home. Please—I don't feel good, I—"

"This will make you feel good," he said quietly.

She could see his face in the half light.

He was smiling.

"Trust me," he murmured, and turned the car off onto a side road.

14

Almost immediately the trees closed in, pressing against the sides of the car, bowing over the roof and shutting out the sky. It was almost like being inside a tunnel, and as Trish stared fearfully out the windshield, the only thing she could see was a tiny stretch of gravel road ahead, illuminated by the headlights.

"Where are we going?" she demanded. She could feel her panic rising until she felt like she was going to explode. She angled herself into the corner of the seat, one hand on the door handle, the other where the seat belt fastened. Storm glanced over at her and frowned.

"Calm down, will you? I don't share this with just anybody, you know. This is a . . . special place."

"Why are you doing this to me?" she blurted out. "I can't stand this—"

Instantly Storm hit the brake, twisting toward her in his seat. In one movement, Trish had the seat belt off and the door open, and without even thinking what she was doing, she tried to run.

She had no idea where she was going.

Still sore from her fall, she struggled through the trees. Branches tore at her face and hair, and clawed at her coat. She heard material ripping and was suddenly aware of something warm on her face and neck—she cried out as her hair snagged on a limb and jerked her head backward. With numb fingers she tried frantically to untangle herself from the trees.

"Trish! *Trish!* Come back here!"

She could hear him behind her, gaining every second. He sounded angry, and in her mind she suddenly heard the whisper—that awful, horrible whisper—*"He is not what he seems to be."*

"Trish!" Storm shouted. "Where the hell are you?"

She gave a final tug and tore her hair free, then staggered off again through the woods. She was numb with cold. Everything felt like it was in slow motion— her legs sank nearly knee-deep in drifts of dead leaves, and her arms flailed uselessly, trying to keep her balance. Without warning she slipped into a hole she hadn't seen and pitched forward onto the ground.

He was on top of her in an instant.

Shrieking, Trish struck out, clawing at his face, grabbing for his hair. She could hear him cursing under his breath and panting for air, and then his sudden surge of strength as he pinned her arms above her head, hard against the ground.

"Stop it!" he yelled at her. "Stop it right now. What are you—crazy?"

"Don't hurt me!" she screamed. "Please let me go—*please!*"

She burst into hysterical tears and felt his hold on

her immediately loosen. Through a haze of panic and terror, she saw his face hovering above her, his expression stunned.

"What is wrong with you?" he mumbled. "What did you think I was going to do?"

She couldn't stop crying. Gasping and sobbing, she tried to sit up and felt his arms go around her, pulling her, then holding her against him.

"Trish," he murmured, "Trish . . . what is it? What's wrong?"

"I—I—please don't—don't do anything to me," she begged. "Just please take me back—"

The silence went on and on. She could feel the roughness of his jacket against her cheek, could smell the soft mustiness of old flannel. When Storm spoke at last, his voice sounded shocked and hurt.

"*Do* something to you? Why would you ever think a thing like that? I would never hurt you, Trish—do you hear me? How could I ever hurt you? What kind of a guy do you think I am, anyway?"

She looked at him then, afraid and confused, not knowing what to think, what to believe. His face looked stony, peering down at her in dismay, his lips pressed tightly together, his eyes suspicious. It was all she could do to keep from screaming again and trying to run, but another part of her wanted to stay— wanted to stay here tight against him and believe that nothing horrible or terrifying had ever happened.

"You can tell me," he said at last, and she could feel her head shaking from side to side, mechanically.

"There's nothing to tell."

"No? I think there must be."

"No." She shook her head again. "No—there really isn't. I'm just—just upset."

"No!" Storm faked surprise, his face finally relaxing into a grin. He reached into his pocket and withdrew a handkerchief, holding it to her nose. "Go ahead. Blow."

Trish did so, then pulled back a little, avoiding his eyes.

"Everything's just been kind of messed up lately."

"Hmmm." Storm gave a noncommittal nod. "But it's nothing you can talk about."

She shook her head. She didn't know what to do, what to say.

"So how good a friend does a guy have to be before you'll trust him with your life?" Storm asked quietly, and Trish's head jerked up.

"Why did you say that?" she demanded. "Why did you say my life?"

"Whoa!" Storm drew back, chuckling, holding her at arm's length. "Down, girl, down. I'm sorry if I picked the wrong cliché. If it makes you that defensive, I won't ask you *anything* about your life, okay?"

"I . . ." Trish shook her head miserably. "I'm just so tired."

"Okay. We've established the fact that I didn't bring you into the woods to"—he cleared his throat suggestively—"take advantage of you." His glance was mischievous. "And since you've tried the cross-country run and found it too treacherous in the woods in the dark, and in your condition—"

Trish could sense a wan smile forming on her lips, yet somehow she didn't feel anything. Storm stood up and gently pulled her to her feet.

"Now—if you have no further objections—could I *please* show you what I brought you here to show you?"

Trish felt herself nodding. She didn't seem to have any control anymore, over her feet, over her mind.

"This way," Storm said gently. He put his arm around her shoulder and gently guided her back to the car. He helped her inside and closed the door, then slid in again beside her.

They drove for another ten minutes, Trish staring dully out the window. It didn't matter that she couldn't see into the night—nothing seemed to be registering much anyway. She was vaguely conscious when the car stopped again and Storm coaxed her out, and then there was the sensation of dead leaves underfoot and the feathery brush of evergreens across her face as she moved through the darkness.

"Where are we going?" It was starting again—that dangerous spark of panic deep inside her—but before she could break free and try to run, Storm stopped abruptly and turned her a little toward the left.

"There," he said softly. "Right over there."

Trish looked. Through a break in the trees she could see a small round clearing, and in the very center, the indistinct outline of what might once have been a cabin, now only leaning walls half standing in a shallow puddle of moonlight.

"What is it?" she murmured, and he laughed softly.

"Use your imagination. It's a house! Well . . . it used to be a house."

"Who does it belong to?"

"Now? Ghosts." He smiled at her. "Come on."

She allowed him to take her hand. Slowly he led her out into the clearing until they were standing alongside what was left of a sagging wooden porch.

"I found this one day when I was out exploring," he explained, his voice almost reverent. "I do that, you know—go out driving and then look for special things no one else has discovered yet." He shrugged. "Of course I know it's only a matter of time before other people show up here when I do, but till then . . ." He took her hand again and urged her forward, but Trish balked.

"Is it safe?"

"Sure. Just don't step on the cracks."

She smiled then. She followed him up onto the wooden platform and in through the open frame of the doorway.

There were only three walls left. The fourth wall, which gave out onto the back of the house, was entirely gone, leaving in its stead a breathtaking view of the small stretch of field, then the underlying valley, bathed in moonglow. Trish drew her breath in sharply.

"It's beautiful. Really."

"I thought you'd think so. Like I said, I wouldn't share this with just anyone."

Trish walked to the back of the cabin and stared out across the nighttime scene below.

"Wouldn't it be wonderful to have a house just like this?"

"I think so," Storm agreed. "What's your house like?"

"Oh, you know." She shrugged evasively. "Just a house."

"Where do you live?"

She started to answer, then closed her mouth again. She ran one hand over the rough logs of the wall and said casually, "Where do *you* live?"

"Me?" The question seemed to have caught him offguard. He took a moment to think. "Across town."

"Where across town?"

"The—uh—Southbrook area."

"You live with your parents?"

"I have . . . an apartment."

"Which apartments? Where?"

Again there was a long silence. He started to speak, cleared his throat, then tried again.

"You know. Those new ones over there."

"Oh." Trish nodded. "The Southbrook apartments. Yes, I know them."

"But this place is so much better," he said quickly. "That's why I love to come here. Sometimes I even pretend it's mine—in good shape, that is."

"I wonder who this place belonged to—do you know?"

"Well . . ." Storm walked a few steps, folded his arms, and leaned gingerly back against a wooden post. "I asked around one time. Seems there's a story that goes with the place—or at least that's what folks around here want you to believe."

"I'd like to hear it."

"It belonged to a woman. She lived here all alone, and it seems she wasn't that popular with the neighbors—not that there were any close by for her to worry about."

Trish turned and looked at him, but his face was bathed in shadows.

"Why? What was wrong with her?"

"Supposedly she was . . . shall we say . . . peculiar." A smile warmed his voice, and he chuckled softly. "Anyway, she had these wild notions that someone was after her. That someone was going to sneak up here to her house during the night and carry her away."

Trish's breath caught in her throat. It was hard for her to get the words out.

"Who? Who was going to come for her?"

"Nobody really knew. Some man, she said. She always mentioned a stranger, but she never said his name."

"Why . . . why did she think he was after her?"

"Who knows?" Storm's foot scraped on the wooden floorboards, and Trish jumped. "Anyway, she hid herself up here and was so scared for so many years that she finally lost her mind."

"She went insane?"

"Well . . . that's what people say. The point is, she just disappeared. Neighbors came up to check on her one day, and she was gone. Vanished. The door was open and a fire was still smoldering in that fireplace over there."

Trish looked toward another wall and saw what remained of a stone hearth.

"They looked and looked—even sent out search parties—but no one ever found her. Some say she went off and killed herself—to get rid of her ghosts once and for all." Storm sighed. "And some say . . ."

"What?" Trish whispered.

"That whoever it was she was so terrified of finally *did* find her after all that time. Found her . . . and murdered her . . . and hid her body so well that no one ever discovered it."

The silence was deep and thick and suffocating. Trish felt her skin crawl, and she burrowed deep, deep into her coat.

"Why are you telling me this?" she murmured.

Storm sounded surprised. "No reason. I just thought you'd be interested in the legend."

"I'd like to go back now."

"Trish . . ."

In one swift movement he'd crossed the room and was next to her, his hands on her shoulders, his head bent low to her own.

"Trish, listen to me. I never would have told you if I'd thought it'd upset you. Come on, it's just an old wives' tale—nobody *really* believes in those anymore."

She tried to pull away, but he only pulled her closer.

"Please!" Her voice rose. "I just want to get out of here."

"Not yet." Storm cut her off, and suddenly he was kissing her, his arms tight around her, pressing her close, and she could feel his lips, warm and soft, tasting hers, trailing down the side of her neck, into the sensitive spot on her shoulder.

"Stop it!"

She slapped him—hard. Gasping in horror at her own reaction, she watched as he recoiled in surprise and lifted one palm to his stinging cheek. For the briefest moment she thought a look of pure rage darkened his eyes—then, just as quickly it was gone, leaving his face shocked and slightly bewildered.

"Take me back," she whispered.

He stepped away, his mouth set in a tight line.

"Okay, lady—you got it."

The ride back to town was one of stony silence. Trish kept her gaze riveted on the window, on the darkness streaming by as Storm sped the car through the chilly streets. As he suddenly turned onto her own street, she faced him in surprise.

"Where are we going?"

"I thought you wanted to go back."

"How did you know I live on this street?"

He sped up again. It was several seconds before he spoke.

"I didn't know this was your street. I was just taking another way to the library."

She was glad when she finally spotted the huge building up ahead. Without another word she jumped out and slammed the door, then raced inside, hovering in the entryway until she was sure his car had faded from view down the street.

I didn't tell him where I lived—did I? Was he really just taking another route to the library?

Steeling herself against the cold, she went out on the street again and took her same shortcuts, ducking through yards and between houses. It was possible, she argued with herself, that Storm *was* telling the truth—it *was* possible to get to the library by taking her street instead of one of the other main roads. Yet something about it just didn't seem quite right.

Such a coincidence that he'd run into her in the library. *I've never noticed him there before tonight.*

She thought about the house in the woods and shuddered. *"She had these wild notions that someone was after her."*

Relieved to reach Nita's block at last, she sneaked into the backyard and up to the porch, letting herself into the kitchen. The house was warm and bright, and with one glance at the clock, she knew someone would be home with her soon. She peeled off her coat and went upstairs to the bedroom.

The room was dark. The only light that came in was from the hallway, and Nita's lamp was off between the beds. Trish saw that she'd forgotten to close the curtains before she'd left. Now she went over and reached up to pull them shut, when something out on the street below made her stop and stare.

It was a car.

It was parked at the curb directly across the street and its headlights were off.

The sputtering glow from a corner streetlamp angled itself down over the car's roof, throwing a pale golden shimmer across the front seat.

And as Trish stood there in the darkness, she could see someone moving.

Gasping, she drew back behind the curtains and watched as a shadow shifted itself behind the steering wheel and then coaxed the engine to life.

Just for the briefest moment she'd caught a glimpse of that face as it turned quickly into the light, then disappeared back into the shadows.

Just for a second, she'd seen him, and she knew she'd seen him before.

It was Wyatt.

15

She didn't turn on the light.

She pressed back against the wall and shut her eyes and tried to think what to do.

What's he doing out there? Why's he watching this house?

She couldn't believe it. It had to be a mistake. *I couldn't really see that clearly. There were shadows— so many shadows. It could have been nothing. The car could have been empty—just a trick of the light, or some neighbor, somebody visiting some neighbor, a stranger.*

"She always mentioned a stranger, but she never said his name . . ."

Trish drew her breath in slowly, held it, let it out. She had to look out that window again—she had to convince herself that she hadn't really seen what she'd thought she'd seen.

She stood at the very edge of the window. The open curtains hid her this way, and she moved one of them and peeked through.

The car was gone.

"Trish!" a voice shouted. "Trish—where are you?"

"Oh, God—Nita!" Trish breathed, then nearly jumped out of her skin as the light snapped on behind her.

"What are you doing standing here in the dark?" Nita regarded her as if she'd gone temporarily insane. "I wanted to call you, but we were so busy I never had a chance! Aren't Mom and Dad home yet? How do you feel?"

Trish nodded and sat down on the edge of Nita's bed. "I'm better. No, they said they'd be late."

"How come you're dressed? I thought you were supposed to stay in bed."

Trish shrugged. "I don't know. I just—"

"Look at you! Were you in another accident or something?"

As Nita came closer and stared at her in disbelief, it suddenly dawned on Trish how she must look after her flight through the woods, after her fight with Storm. She shook her head and tried to think of something to say, but Nita rushed on.

"You have all these scratches on your face—and your *hair!* And there's dried blood on your neck! And look at your bandage. Don't tell me you pulled out the stitches—"

"The stitches are fine," Trish assured her, though she put up her hand gingerly just to make sure. "I—Don't tell your mom, okay—she's been so worried about me. I just had to get out for a while and get some fresh air. So I went down the block—and—and this dog started chasing me—and so I cut through some of the neighbors' yards and I fell into the bushes—"

"Oh, poor Trish!" Nita groaned, taking Trish into her arms and hugging her tightly. "Have you ever had a week so awful as the one you're having now?"

Trish shook her head and said nothing, and Nita immediately pushed her toward the hallway.

"Go in the bathroom and clean up—then get that nightgown on and climb in bed. I'll bring you some cocoa and some of that chocolate cake Mom made yesterday, and then I want you to go right to sleep and—"

"Yes, Mother." Trish tried to make a joke, but could hardly bring herself to smile. "Nita—"

"Hmmm?"

"Did you see a car outside when you came home?"

"What kind of car?"

"I don't know. An old one."

Nita shook her head. "Nope. Why? Are you expecting someone?"

She didn't notice that Trish didn't laugh. She hurried downstairs to fix their snacks, and uneasily, Trish got ready for bed.

They were still sitting up talking when Imogene came home. She stood in the doorway and stared hard at Trish, squinting through her glasses.

"I can't say it's the best you've ever looked," she said truthfully.

"You missed all the excitement." Nita grinned. "Trish went out and got attacked by a dog."

"Anyone I know?" Imogene asked.

"And how come *you're* home so late?" Nita asked, tossing a pillow at her head.

"I went to another movie. That filmfest they're having at the mall is really very enlightening."

"Enlightening." Nita nodded at Trish, trying to keep a straight face. "Enlightening, don't you know."

"You should go. Interesting people show up there."

"What kind of interesting people?"

"Wyatt's been there," Imogene said, and Nita glanced at her sharply.

"You're lying."

"I'm not," Imogene declared solemnly. "And since he's turned out to be your new project, maybe you should start hanging out where he hangs out."

"What kind of movies was he seeing?" Nita asked curiously. "Horror? Race cars? No—I know—science fiction?"

"Wrong," Imogene said smugly. "Old romance classics."

Nita's mouth fell open. "Now I know you're lying."

"I most certainly am not. He went the whole week the filmfest was going on. You've got to start learning about men, sister dear. Still waters often run very, very deep."

Trish looked troubled, but managed to keep her thoughts to herself. *It couldn't have been Wyatt outside in that car.*

"Romances." Nita shook her head in awe. "Who would ever have figured? He looks so . . . so . . ."

"Manly," Imogene's tone was matter of fact. "I think he looks quite manly and resilient."

"And he acts so . . ."

"Self-sufficient. I like that in a man, don't you?"

Nita looked uncertain. "I'm not sure. I still think he's weird."

"Well, the feeling's probably mutual." Imogene couldn't hold back a smile. "So does anyone care to join me for a movie this weekend?" She glanced over at Trish. "Trish—are you nodding off over there?"

"If she's not, she should be," Nita said sternly. "We shouldn't be keeping her up when she needs to rest." She took a quick sip of cocoa, then added, "Oh, I almost forgot, Trish—Bethany wasn't at work today."

Trish looked blank. "What? You're kidding."

"Maybe they fired her," Imogene said dryly.

"I don't think so." Nita set her cup on the nightstand. "I mean, if they did, nobody seemed to know anything about it. See, here's the thing. She was *supposed* to be there, but she never showed up."

"That's impossible. Bethany would show up for work even if the world were ending." Trish tried to laugh, but it sounded thin and nervous.

"Well, something must have *happened* to her then," Nita said offhandedly. "Because she sure wasn't there tonight. Some of the kids in The Eatery were asking about you, and they said they hoped she *never* came back. I swear—*nobody* likes that girl. They should just get rid of her."

A cold, inexplicable chill snaked its way up Trish's spine. She shivered and hugged her pillow to her chest.

"Cold?" Nita asked. "Imogene, turn up the heat, will you?"

"Well, you didn't miss much at school," Imogene said, as Trish stared down at her hands in her lap. "This is a good week not to go—there's nothing happening."

"But I'll be there tomorrow," Trish said, and they both looked at her in surprise.

"You most certainly will not," Nita informed her. "Not in your condition."

"There's nothing wrong with my condition," Trish said, but her voice was hesitant, her brow furrowed in thought. *What was it?* She could almost remember something that Storm had said earlier—something about Bethany. *"I doubt if she'll be there much longer."*

"Trish?" Nita waved one hand in front of her friend's face. "Hello? Anyone home?"

"I'm sorry, Nita, I—"

"No school. And no work."

"Yes, work." Trish glanced quickly down to keep Nita and Imogene from reading the alarm in her eyes. "I have to go to work." *I have to show up at the mall. You don't have any idea how much I have to show up at the mall.*

"Why put yourself through all that?" Nita groaned. "It would have been okay today, 'cause Bethany wasn't there. But what if she's back tomorrow?"

And what was it—*something else*—that night in the stockroom. The guard had been talking . . . *"She's not nice to you . . . she makes you unhappy."*

"You can't go," Nita said again.

"I'm going," Trish told her.

"You're brain dead," Imogene said bluntly. "Goodnight."

"Trish," Nita began, but Trish scooted down under the covers and flipped off the lamp.

"I *have* to go to work tomorrow, Nita. It's very . . . important."

"What's more important than your health?"

Your *health*, Trish wanted to tell her. *All of our health. All of our lives.* But instead she said, "Goodnight, Nita," and pulled the blankets up over her head.

She lay there a long, long time, unable to sleep.

She kept listening for the sound of a car cruising slowly by in the night.

Troubled and restless, she finally got up and stood

beside the window, staring mournfully out into the darkness. She could hear Nita breathing deeply and slowly in her bed, lost in the wonderful oblivion of some dream.

Trish wondered if she'd ever be able to sleep like that again.

She watched the sun rise, and when the alarm went off, she just managed to slide back into bed before Nita woke up. She was glad Nita was so incoherent in the morning—her friend hardly noticed that Trish was being unusually quiet and unresponsive. Against Mrs. Hanson's better judgment, she insisted on going to school and asked Nita and Imogene to drop her off at the gas station to pick up her car. She promised to meet them in the usual place for lunch, then waved as they went on without her.

Her car was parked outside, and after paying and getting her keys, she climbed in and started off. She didn't understand exactly what had been wrong with it—something electrical, the man had told her—and she made a mental note to tell her mother when she got back from her trip. She rode for several miles, then suddenly realized she'd spent the whole time glancing out the windows and into the rearview mirror.

You really are paranoid today, aren't you? You better get hold of yourself before you have a wreck or something.

She glanced down at the seat beside her and saw a cassette lying there. Picking it up, she examined it briefly, then frowned—it didn't have a label, and she couldn't remember what kind of music it was. She stuck it into the tape deck and turned up the volume, hoping it was another of Imogene's classical surprises. She could do with a little soothing right now.

But it wasn't music that came blasting from the

speakers, filling the car—her head—her heart—with sudden terror.

"You're a naughty girl, Trish," the voice whispered, yet it was so loud, like a shout, a scream in the close confines of the car, and Trish's hands jerked on the steering wheel as her eyes fastened on the tape deck in unbelieving horror.

"Naughty girl," the voice went on, and he was angry with her—she could hear it, she could *feel* it, as if he were here with her right now, able to see her helplessness and her fear.

"I told you not to talk to anyone. I told you not to *tell* anyone."

"But I didn't!" she screamed, even though she was alone, even though she knew he couldn't *really* hear her—could he? "I didn't tell *anyone!* I *didn't!"*

"You can't have anyone else, Trish, do you understand? Only me. *Only me!"*

The voice was hard now, cold and hard and dangerous, and Trish saw the red glow of a stoplight as she drove right through it—saw a woman's shocked face as she barely missed hitting her car.

"Stop it!" she shrieked. *"Stop it!* Why are you *doing* this?"

"Only me, Trish," and he was mumbling now, rambling, as if his thoughts had gone suddenly out of control. "No one else. Do you hear me? No one else. There can't be. I tried to tell you that before . . . I tried to make you see. No one . . . no one ever."

He paused then, as if trying to get himself under control. When at last he spoke, his voice was honey-sweet. "Well . . . I *did* try to warn you, didn't I? But you wouldn't listen. So now . . . now I have to show you how *serious* I am."

"No . . . no . . ."

"You'd better be at the mall today, Trish—do you hear me? You'd better be there at the mall."

"But why—why are you—"

"I'm the one you belong to, do you understand? *I'm* the one who loves you! We're *destined,* you and I—we're *meant* to be together, Trish. And *no one* else can have you!"

She felt a jolt as her car ran up onto the curb. She slammed on the brake and put her hands over her face, shaking uncontrollably, hunching down in the seat, knowing that no matter where she was, where she ran, she couldn't hide from him.

"You're mine, Trish," he whispered lovingly. "And tonight we'll finally be together. *Forever.*"

16

She thought she was losing her mind.

For several minutes Trish just sat there in her car, rocking back and forth, her arms wrapped tightly around herself. *What am I going to do? I have to tell someone—I have to—but I can't. He'll find out—he'll hurt my friends. What did he mean, he's going to show me how serious he is? What's he going to do now?*

She was scarcely even aware when she turned the car back onto the street, when she picked up speed, when she turned in the direction away from school and sped across town.

Southbrook. That's where he said he lived, didn't he? The apartments in Southbrook.

Storm. She didn't know why she was thinking of him now—last night she couldn't wait to get away from him.

And yet she'd never felt so desperate. She'd never felt so utterly alone, and in her panic, all she could think about was getting away—far, far away where that horrible voice would never find her. She would go to Storm's apartment, but she wouldn't go in. She wouldn't even knock on his door. She'd just sit outside in the car for a while, just until she calmed down, and then just knowing that someone else was there nearby, inside the building, would make her feel better.

Why am I doing this? I don't know why I'm doing this.

She wasn't thinking straight—she wasn't sure *what* she was doing anymore. As she screeched to a halt outside the Southbrook apartment building, she jumped out of the car and ran through the front entrance, stopping at the mailboxes in the hall, frantically scanning the names posted above them.

There were six names there.

None of them was Storm's.

Bewildered, Trish went over them again, slowly, one by one.

She sagged back against the wall and forced herself to take a deep, steadying breath. *Why did I come here anyway? Athan probably knows I came here—he's probably outside watching me right now—following me wherever I go—and now Storm's in danger, too, and it's all my fault.*

She couldn't believe she'd been so stupid, so careless. She started to cry, then stopped herself at once, hurrying back outside, getting in her car. She didn't know where to go, where to run. School was out of the question—she'd be worthless there. And she couldn't go home—Athan knew where she lived. She didn't want to go to the mall, but she knew she'd have to go back sometime. And maybe if she went now, it would appease him somehow—appease him for her making a stupid mistake and coming here to Storm's—and then he would leave everyone alone.

She was sure she was being followed. More than once she took a sudden turnoff and cut through a little-traveled side street, and she could swear that a car was tailing her, far behind her in the distance. She wondered if her car was bugged. She wondered if someone was hiding in her trunk. She even pulled off the road once to look, then squatted down to check underneath the car, in case Athan had managed somehow to hide himself up between the wheels.

I'm totally losing it.

She drove to the mall. She parked her car in the employee lot and walked through the main entrance and went straight to The Eatery. None of the stores were open yet, but the food stands were already beginning their preparations for the day. Trish recognized a few of the people working the day shift, but Bethany wasn't among them. She checked out Pizza Park, but Storm didn't seem to be working. She was surprised to see Wyatt cleaning off tables, and for a few minutes she just stood and stared at him. He must have sensed someone watching him—it wasn't long before he looked up and met her eyes straight on. Trish steeled herself and walked over.

"Hi," she said.

He gave a nod and grunted.

"I didn't know you worked the day shift."

"Sometimes." He shrugged. "I'm . . . filling in for a buddy of mine."

"You know, it's kind of funny," Trish went on, plunging right in. "Last night I thought I saw you."

Wyatt scratched the side of his head. "Where was I?"

"Outside my friend's house."

Wyatt's face never changed expression. He shrugged again and flicked his rag over the tabletop.

"Yeah? Weird."

"It is weird. He really looked like you."

"Wow. Two of us. Can the world stand it?"

"*Was* it you?" she asked bluntly.

Wyatt leaned over and moved a chair. He wrung out his rag and wiped again in slow, wide circles.

"Probably not. What was I doing?"

"Sitting in a car."

"Then I guess it wasn't me." Wyatt looked uninterested. "My car got stolen. Remember?"

Trish stared at him. His eyes slid away, lingered on a spot of spilled ketchup. Slowly he reached down, wiped it up in one quick smear, then just as slowly turned his attention back to her again.

"That must have been some accident you had."

Trish frowned. "How did *you* know about my accident?"

"Everyone knows about that." He started to move off, then glanced back at her over his shoulder. "If I were you," he said, his eyes narrowing, "next time . . . I'd take the stairs."

Trish bought a cup of coffee and sat down at a table. When the doors of the mall opened at ten, the place filled rapidly with Friday shoppers and the Sidewalk Sale officially began. *How strange that I'm sitting here surrounded by all these people and I'm in more danger than I've ever been before.* She didn't know what she was supposed to do—wait to hear from Athan again? Wait until something happened to one of her friends? Remembering the voice on the tape made Trish shudder—it hadn't sounded like a warning this time.

He was dead serious.

Why did I bother to go to Storm's apartment? Especially after Athan told me not to talk to anyone? I don't know what I was thinking. Athan probably saw me—maybe Storm isn't here because Athan did something to him.

A surge of panic came up in her throat. Swallowing hard, she tried to choke it back down, gripping her chair with both hands.

Why wasn't Storm's name by the mailboxes? He must have been confused about the apartments. I must have gone to the wrong place. Maybe someone else will be in danger now because Athan thinks I talked to someone in that building.

She couldn't stand to think about that possibility. She leaned over the table and cradled her head in her arms.

And what about Wyatt—he said he didn't even have a car, so that couldn't have been him outside Nita's house last night. Why did I think it was him? I hardly even know the guy. Nita's right—he is strange. What could he possibly have to do with me anyway?

Trish forced herself to get up and walk. She went entirely through the first level of the mall, and then up to the second, and then to the third. It seemed like every shopper was watching her. She felt hidden eyes peering out from each doorway, from behind every display window. Even the mannequins looked too frighteningly lifelike. *He could be anywhere . . . he could be anyone. . . .*

As the morning wore on into afternoon, it was obvious that things were as normal as they could be. She saw employees she knew, she saw the elderly security guard trying to comfort a lost child—she even spotted Roger talking to the girl at the information booth. She was still embarrassed by her earlier confrontation with him, but he didn't seem to notice her, so she walked on.

By three she was exhausted. She tried to convince herself that this was what Athan had had in mind all along—not really hurting anybody, but making her suffer the apprehension of *wondering* if he would hurt anybody. She knew Nita and Imogene would get there soon, and she spent the rest of the time trying to concoct a believable story as to why she hadn't gone to school this morning after all.

She didn't want to face them right now; she just wanted to be left alone. She went back to Muffin-Mania and slipped into her apron and began doing some work in back, but Bethany still hadn't showed up. There was no doubt that the other kids who worked there were delighted at their manager's absence—Trish couldn't remember when the atmosphere had been as fun and relaxed since she'd started her job.

She wasn't surprised when Nita came by before going upstairs—she made up some story about going back to her own house and resting that morning, and the lie seemed to satisfy Nita.

"But you still look terrible," Nita scolded her. "Promise me you'll stay over tonight and really get some rest."

"Yes, yes, I promise—"

"Oh—and here's your flashlight. I keep forgetting to give it back to you."

"I thought you'd want to keep it. You handled it so well when Wyatt tried to attack us in the parking lot."

"Very funny. I don't know why you bother with it anyway—the light's so bad."

"Well"—Trish shrugged—"it's better than nothing, I guess."

"And speaking of Wyatt, I've decided to revise my attack plan. I'm going to be so irresistible to him that he'll be eating right out of my hand."

"Maybe you should settle for him washing his jacket."

"You're right. He is quirky. I like that."

And slippery, Trish wanted to say. *Like you never quite know if you should believe him or not.*

They promised to have dinner together, and Trish breathed a sigh of relief when her friend went upstairs to work.

The Eatery was exceptionally busy that afternoon, and as the hours wore on into evening, Trish was relieved to have her hands full with no time to think of other things. Once she glanced up from making change and thought she saw Storm over in the pizza stand, but when she looked up again, he wasn't there. She looked briefly around the snack area for Wyatt, but he seemed to have disappeared.

The endlessly long line of hungry customers was just beginning to wind down when one of the other workers called Trish into the back.

"You got a phone call," the girl said, looking slightly puzzled, as Trish reached over to pick up the receiver. "No—I mean, they already hung up."

Nita, Trish thought instantly—Nita was probably going to be late for her dinner break and didn't want Trish to wait for her. "What did they want?"

"Well." The girl frowned. "She said she was a friend of yours, but I could hardly hear her. She sounded like she had a terrible cold."

Trish stared at the phone, not saying anything.

"I told her you were right here, but she just hung up before I could get you," the girl complained.

"That's okay," Trish mumbled. "Did she say her name? Do you remember? Was it Nita?"

The girl thought a moment, then shook her head. "No . . . it didn't sound like Nita. It sounded like . . . Emily? Emmeline?"

"Imogene," Trish whispered. "Oh, no."

"Imogene?" The girl sounded it out loud. "Well, maybe. Like I said—"

"What else did she say?"

The girl shrugged, looking a little ashamed. "Something about—I don't know—a matter of life and death? I mean, I tried to call you but—"

"Where is she?" Trish broke in, but the girl was going on, trying to explain.

"And there might have been more, but I couldn't make out everything she was saying. She sounded so hoarse, she could hardly whisper. Her voice was real deep and low and—"

"Life and death," Trish echoed. She was rigid now, stiff and staring and clenching her fists and trying not to fall apart right here in the hot stuffy little room.

"And she said for you to hurry—"

"Where?" Trish demanded. "Where *is* she?"

"I don't know." The girl shrugged apologetically and shook her head. "She didn't say where—she just said—" The girl closed her eyes, thinking hard. "She just said, 'Tell her to come now—before it's too late.'"

17

Trish didn't stop to explain. With a strangled cry she shoved the girl aside and took off for the bookstore.

Imogene—not Imogene!

There were people everywhere. Extra tables of special bargains had been set up outside every store, slowing pedestrian traffic to a near standstill, and as Trish tried to shove her way through the crowds, it was all she could do to keep from knocking shoppers to the ground. As she spied the bookstore up ahead, she craned her neck, hoping to catch sight of Imogene, but there were too many bodies crushed together, too many lines, and she couldn't see a thing. She broke through the bottleneck of people at last and squeezed her way up to one of the counters, ignoring the angry looks from the other people in line.

"Imogene," she said breathlessly. "Imogene Hanson."

"I'll be glad to wait on you when I finish with these other customers first," the salesman said icily.

Trish leaned forward over the counter and grabbed his arm.

"No—you don't understand—it's an emergency! I need to see Imogene."

Rolling his eyes, the clerk nodded and excused himself, working his way to the rear of the store. He opened the door of the office and poked his head in, and after a brief conversation with someone inside, he turned and shook his head at Trish.

"Imogene's not here."

"Well, where is she?"

"How should I know?" he said grumpily. "Maybe she went on break."

"This is really important. Don't you have any way of—"

"Look, I have to finish with these people out here, or we're gonna have a riot on our hands." He frowned at her and stalked back to the front.

Trish stood there helplessly, not knowing what to do. Her first instinct was to go get Nita, but she didn't want to panic her friend. She looked desperately around the crowded store until she spotted another salesgirl shelving books on the far wall.

"Excuse me." Trish ran up to her. "I've got to find Imogene Hanson—do you know where she is?"

The girl nodded and wiped a weary hand across her brow. "Can you believe this mess? Thank goodness I've got the rest of the weekend off!"

"Imogene," Trish prompted her. "It's important."

"She's not here," the girl said. "She had to leave the store for a while, but she should be back in—I don't know—twenty minutes or so?"

155

"Where'd she go?" Trish persisted. "I'm a good friend of hers—it's really an emergency—"

"Something about an invoice." The girl shrugged. "A mixed-up delivery of some kind."

Trish stared at her, her mind reeling.

"Someone called from the loading dock and asked for Imogene. So I imagine that's where she is."

"And you—you talked to this person?"

She nodded. "Yeah. It wasn't the usual guy who always calls us about a mix-up, though. I'd never heard this guy's voice before. Hard to understand—like maybe he had a cold."

"How long ago did she leave?"

"Oh . . ." The girl glanced at her watch and then at the clock on the wall. "About ten minutes ago, maybe? She had to go straighten out some problem about a wrong book shipment or something like that. Personally, I don't know what a book delivery is doing coming in here this late in the day—and especially at a crazy time like this. They could at least have waited till morning!"

"Thanks!" Trish gasped. "Thanks a lot!"

There was no way she could go to Nita now—no way she could let her know what was happening. *Oh, Imogene—please! I hope I'm not too late!*

Trish made her way to the service elevator, praying that someone else would be going in her direction. The elevator came at once, but she was alone, and reluctantly she pushed the button to go down. What was it about elevators that was so unsettling, she found herself wondering—especially at night, especially when you were all by yourself. Huddling back in the corner, she counted to herself as the floors went by. *Get out here on the basement level. But then I have to take another elevator.*

She dreaded this part of the journey more than anything else—the scary freight elevator that would take her the rest of the way down. For a moment she stood before it, gathering her courage. Then, swallowing her fear, she moved forward and peeked cautiously into the dim recesses of its interior.

Empty.

Slipping inside, she pushed the button, grimacing as the old door rattled sideways and shut her in. She tried to concentrate on what she would do once she reached the loading docks, tried not to think about how frightened she was as the elevator began to lurch and sway its way deep into the bowels of the building.

The whole car shook as if it were barely holding together. She found herself wondering just how old the cables were that supported it, just how sturdy the shivering walls and floor and ceiling, just how deep the shaft. She felt vulnerable even thinking about it and pressed herself back into the corner as the elevator shook and shimmied around her. She kept seeing Imogene's face, those round, wise eyes behind their glasses, and Trish bit her own lip to keep back tears. *Just a few more floors and I'll be there—just a few more floors and I'll be on solid ground and Imogene will probably be waiting right outside the elevator, wondering why I came all this way over here to find her.*

The elevator hit bottom with a dull thud, bouncing a few times as if it couldn't make up its mind to stop. Trish held her breath as the door jerked open and then slid back with a rusty groan. The sound echoed on and on for several seconds—and then there was silence.

Trish hurried out, glancing nervously back over her shoulder, going deeper and deeper into the gloomy passageway that wound and twisted toward the warehouse. Was anyone even still working down here tonight? She had no idea what kinds of hours the people at the docks kept—for all she knew, maybe the warehouse was locked up tight for the night. But Imogene probably wouldn't even be thinking about that, Trish worried—she'd have no reason to suspect a thing. *Because she doesn't know what's going on—no one knows—only me.*

There wasn't a soul around. As Trish walked faster, the sound of her footsteps echoed eerily off the damp walls, filling the tunnel, as if other footsteps were following.

Or were those other footsteps real?

Trish froze, her heart pounding.

The footsteps stopped.

She took a cautious step. Another. Then another.

The only footsteps were her own.

She didn't realize she'd been holding her breath until she let it out in a long sigh. She cast another nervous glance around and continued on.

Ahead of her the passageway suddenly curved off to the right. As Trish got near it, she began to slow down . . . then frowned, and stopped. It was silly, she knew, but all at once she didn't *want* to go around that curve—didn't want to see what was on the other side.

Panicking, she backed up a little, her mind in a spin. *I have to go on—I have to find Imogene.* And yet, for just one split instant, she'd had the unmistakable feeling that she shouldn't go around that curve.

That something was waiting for her on the other side of the wall.

Her blood froze in her veins. She tried to take another step, but her feet were rooted to the floor. The corridor was thick with silence and shadows, yet as her terrified eyes swept slowly in each direction, she sensed somehow that she wasn't alone.

Oh, no! No—

Something stirred ahead of her. A faint rustling sound . . . a *sliding* sound . . . like a foot . . . dragging across the floor.

Her eyes were riveted on the curve of the tunnel.

She knew with chilling certainty now that something was hiding there.

Coming closer.

No . . . please—

The air seemed to darken, shadows shifting and gathering and taking fearful shape into something solid.

Something human. . . .

And suddenly she saw the outline of a face—

An arm—reaching—

And as his hand groped out into the sickly light, she saw the ice pick—the blood dripping thickly onto the floor.

With a scream, Trish whirled and took off for the elevator.

18

He was behind her.

She could hear him calling her name—his whisper hoarse and loud as it echoed eerily off the walls. She could hear his feet, stumbling and uneven, gaining on her—closer—closer—

Ice pick—blood—sickening, gruesome images pelted her brain, and she could hardly see where she was going. *Someone hurt behind that wall—someone dead. Oh, Imogene—Imogene—*

Sobbing, she wound through the tunnels, praying the elevator would still be there, knowing that everything in her life now depended on mere seconds of time. *I've got to get help—got to find someone. But who—who can I tell? Who can I trust? It might be Nita next—if I tell, it might be Nita—*

For all she knew Nita was already in danger—for all she knew Nita's life could be at stake right at this very second—*oh, God, what am I going to do?*

When she saw the door yawning wide at the end of the hall, she fell inside and slammed herself in, but she could still *hear* him—his muffled, frantic cries, over and over through the empty corridors, the beating of his fists as the elevator started up.

She was shaking so badly, she could hardly stand. Her heart thudded in her chest and threatened to explode. As the elevator continued its slow climb, she had to force herself to move, to reach out for the controls. *What if he's out there when the doors open? What if he's waiting for me?*

She saw the numbers go by in the directory above the door.

She saw her floor appear at last, and she breathed a sigh of relief.

The elevator kept going.

Puzzled, she hit the car-station panel, but nothing happened. She banged on it with her fist and looked desperately around for an alarm button. She pressed the emergency stop, but the car kept going. Spotting a recessed telephone, she picked it up and began to yell for help.

The line was silent.

As the elevator kept going up, she could feel her fears rising with it, icy terror creeping over her body. *What's happening with this thing?* She beat again on the floor selector and screamed loudly, but her cries only echoed back, mocking her.

And then, without warning, the elevator stopped.

As Trish watched in terror, the door shuddered— began to slide open.

"No! *No!* Stay *away* from me!"

She threw herself on the CLOSE button and pushed until her arms ached from the strain. *No . . . no . . . please, no.* She could see something trying to get in—something dark and shadowy trying to work its way into the narrow crack—and she pushed harder, sobbing under her breath. The door trembled again—once—then slid shut. *He's out there—I know he's out there. Oh, God, what'll I do?*

She started beating on the panel. *Go! Go! I can't stay here—I have to get out!*

Nothing happened.

Trish stopped—stood there listening. She felt her knees give out, and she slid down into a heap on the floor.

The elevator started back down.

It was nothing. Someone else pushed the button on some other floor, then they changed their mind. That's all it was—it was nothing . . . nothing. . . . Her chest heaved convulsively, and as she watched the numbers go by, she realized that she'd passed her floor again.

Jumping up, she reached out frantically for the buttons. The elevator jerked to a halt, throwing her back against the wall.

D level. The floor that led to the loading docks.

The level she'd just escaped from.

She was terrified to open the door. She was terrified not to. She couldn't get out here—she *couldn't!*—couldn't take that chance of *him* being out there.

The door started to open. Trish slammed her fist on the CLOSE button and waited. The door stopped. Moved back again. *There must be some stairs down here—emergency stairs. If I could just get out and find the stairs and get back to the main floor.*

She had to do it. She had to get out of here—she couldn't stand being in here another minute.

She felt sweat trickling down the sides of her face. She felt the icy prickle of fear gripping her spine. Slowly . . . slowly . . . she started to push OPEN.

The elevator started moving.

"No! No! Let me out of here!" Screaming, Trish began hitting the panel once again. She didn't care where she stopped now—any floor—*any floor*. She just had to get out. She felt like the walls were closing in on her, swallowing her alive. She couldn't breathe —couldn't *breathe*—

He's doing this. She was sure of it now, and her fear and hatred rose up in her throat, choking her even more. *He's doing this and he's out there somewhere and he's playing with me like a mouse in a cage. He's playing with me—and he's enjoying it—*

The sudden jolt threw her into the wall.

As Trish got back to her feet, she saw that she was stopped at B level—exactly where she wanted to go. Sobbing gratefully, she rushed forward and waited for the door to open.

Nothing happened.

Puzzled, she pushed the button. Pushed it again. The doors stayed closed.

Panicking once more, she hit OPEN—EMERGENCY— every button on the whole panel. *No—no—this can't be happening!*

The door shuddered violently—jerked—hesitated. She wedged her hands into the crack and tried to pull, groaning at the effort.

It opened a little farther, then seemed to stick.

Damn! What is wrong with this stupid thing? Gritting her teeth, Trish put all her strength into yet another tug, but the door wouldn't budge. She was beside herself—frantic to escape. *I have to get back to the mall—back to Nita—to find help—back with people where I can hide.* She pounded on the door, kicking it, slamming it with her shoulder till her body screamed with pain. *I've got to get out—I've got to get out of here!*

She didn't expect it to burst open so suddenly.

Jumping back in alarm, she watched as the door trundled sideways and clattered to a stop.

To her dismay she saw the elevator had missed the floor by three feet. To get out now she would have to climb up.

She stared at the opening in front of her.

And afterward, she never really knew exactly *what* it was that had stopped her from climbing out—that had stopped her from going out through that door at that precise moment.

For suddenly—something fell into the doorway and hung there—blocking her escape—swinging back and forth—slowly—from the roof of the elevator.

And as her eyes widened in horror, the thing slipped down a little more . . . swaying gently . . . right in front of her face . . .

It was an arm.

She could see the sleeve—what was left of it— savagely shredded and stiff with dried blood— plastered to the red, red skin beneath. . . .

And she could see the puncture wounds—swollen and clotted shut—running the whole length of the arm.

And she could smell the thick, thick stench of death.

Gagging, Trish stumbled backward, her stomach heaving, her mind screaming with panic.

The arm slipped a little more.

It jerked, as if trying to grab hold of her—

And as the head fell down like a broken puppet and gazed at her upside down, Trish recognized the face at once—the hair matted with blood, the features smeared with blood, blood, and more blood, the sightless eyes staring and pleading and terrified, the handle of the ice pick wedged deep into her throat.

"No," Trish murmured. "Bethany . . ."

And even from the back of the elevator, she could see the piece of soiled, smeared paper on Bethany's neck—pinned in place by the ice pick—and she could read the words slashed there in dripping red letters.

YOU'RE LUCKY. THIS COULD HAVE BEEN IMOGENE.

19

The world ran together in shades of red.

For an endless moment Trish seemed to be standing outside herself, watching a gruesome scene in her worst imaginable nightmare. But then, as reality began to seep back, she was vaguely aware of her body moving sideways . . . inching around the inner walls of the car . . . heading toward the door . . . toward escape.

She would have to go right past Bethany.

She would have to hoist herself up into that tiny narrow opening between the door and the body— and maybe that hand would touch her, maybe that hand would brush her arm as she went by, or maybe that head would rub against her shoulder and the eyes would stare accusingly up into her own face.

Trish paused beside the body.

She drew in her breath and started to climb out.

There was a sudden rush of sound as the body toppled onto the floor, crumpling itself into a bloody heap.

Bethany's arm flailed out and slid down the side of her leg.

With a shriek, Trish jumped back and got the door closed—pounding on the buttons, crying, begging, only no one was there to hear, to save her. She could feel the elevator bouncing slightly, only she wasn't *moving*—no numbers were changing on the directory —and as the car swayed and jerked once more, she molded herself into one corner and raised terrified eyes to the ceiling.

He's on top of the elevator!

She *knew* he was there—she was *sure* of it—and as she stared, transfixed, at the emergency exit, the car finally started to move again, going up and up, numbers flying past in an incoherent blur. She was babbling, sobbing with terror. He was *up* there, just on the other side of that door in the ceiling, and she was trapped, *trapped and helpless*.

For a second it actually felt like she was slowing down.

Gasping for breath, she reached weakly for the handrail, propping herself against the wall. And when she finally realized what was happening—when the sudden, awful realization stabbed into her brain—it was too late even to cry for help.

There was just that instant of hesitation—that fleeting instant of hope.

And then the horrible rushing beneath her— around her.

The vast, empty nothingness of plummeting down and down and down forever.

In her last moment of consciousness, Trish knew the elevator was falling.

And she felt sad, somehow, for the way she was going to die.

20

Death was a dream.

Trish was only vaguely aware of sensations as she drifted . . . close to waking . . . then lost again in deep, deep sleep.

Death was a warm, oblivious dream, and as she hovered once more on the very edge of light, she heard the soft sound of moaning—sensed pain and great danger—and tried to recoil again into her tight cocoon of darkness.

"Help me," someone murmured, and then she realized it was her own voice she was hearing—her own weak voice calling out in the deep, empty silence.

Groggily, Trish moved her head—cried out in pain—lay very still.

She could see only darkness around her, and there was something hard beneath her cheek. She could feel her muscles straining and suddenly realized that she was lying down and that her face was stuck to the floor.

"What . . . where . . ."

She forced herself to move again, ignoring the dull throbbing pain that rushed through her. Slowly her cheek pulled free, and she saw dim light and four dark walls enclosing her.

I'm in some kind of cage.

No—I'm still inside the elevator.

Confused and shaken, Trish stumbled to her feet and leaned heavily against the wall. She could see a number illuminated in the directory above the door—D level—the floor with the loading docks. *So I didn't fall and hit bottom—so I didn't die after all. It was just another game—just another game.* She groped for the panel, trying to find the one button that would get her back to the basement level.

She pushed it.

The elevator began to rise.

She saw the B appear in the directory window, and she was afraid to believe it, afraid to hope that she'd really made it this time.

The door slid open.

The basement lay before her, bathed in heavy shadows.

She peered out the door—saw the short hallway, the second elevator waiting for her at the other end.

She walked out and heard the door shut behind her. She started forward, her pain now greater than her fear, her mind fuzzy and bewildered. *What happened to me? How long have I been out?*

She only knew she had to get back to the mall. *In a few minutes I'll remember everything and I can think what to do. I just have to get back—have to get help.*

Bethany.

170

The memory hit her like a cold shock. As the elevator opened up onto the main floor of the mall, Trish stood there and stared.

The mall was empty.

The corridors were dimmed . . . the shopfronts were closed and dark.

I must be locked in. . . .

For a long moment Trish stood there, her mind a blank. On every side of her, hallways and corridors stretched endlessly into nothingness. Above her, each new level seemed to hang, dreamlike and suspended, like the painted backdrop to a ghostly play. It was so quiet—so unnaturally still. Everything seemed frozen, as if somehow, while she'd been away, time had stopped, and all the people in the world had simply vanished.

Trish turned slowly, taking a long, careful look around her. *I'll just let myself out. Somewhere. If the alarm goes off, I'll just . . .*

What?

Immediately she was filled with a cold sense of dread. What *could* she do? Tell the police she'd gotten sick and fainted? Gotten locked in? They'd want to know *how*—and then she'd look suspicious, like a shoplifter who'd lost her nerve and gotten caught. Tell them about Bethany? Tell them she'd accidentally gotten locked in with a dead girl? But of course he would have moved her by now—of course the body would have conveniently disappeared—just like that other one. They'd *never* believe her—she'd be in more trouble than she'd ever been in her whole life.

But how *could* it get any worse, really?

There's a murderer after me . . . after my friends. How could it possibly get any worse?

Slowly she started walking. This was no accident

that she was locked in here—that she'd been imprisoned in that elevator until after closing time.

"Tonight we'll finally be together . . . forever."

She heard his whisper again in her mind—in the quick, fearful beating of her heart. *But was it only in my mind—or did it come from that doorway there, or that window over there, or . . .*

Trish began to run. She stumbled down the nearest corridor and threw herself against the exit doors, beating on them, pounding the glass with her fists.

"Let me out!" Trish screamed. "Please—someone —let me out of here!"

The doors were locked; she couldn't get them open. She turned and put her back against them, facing the empty hallway like a trapped animal.

"Please," Trish whispered. "Oh, please, I've got to get away."

Awkwardly she retraced her steps, then turned down another wing of the mall. At the end of the hallway she could see the parking lot stretching out beyond the doors—freedom so close yet so impossibly far away—and again she beat on the glass and screamed for help. Panic rising, she turned back and headed for another exit—then another—and still another—each one a dead end. As she stopped to catch her breath, she suddenly spotted some pay phones and went over to grab one of them up.

"Hello? Operator? Can someone hear me?"

She was pushing the buttons over and over again— 911—911—waiting to hear a calming voice, trying to tell them to come and get her, to come and help, when suddenly she jerked the receiver away and saw the sawed-off cord dangling from the end.

"No . . . no. . . ."

She tried all of them then, groping madly from one

to the other, snatching them up, throwing them down. Every single phone line had been cut.

As she flung the last one in despair, she watched it skid across the floor—heard the clatter echoing over and over again.

Stupid—stupid! He knows right where you are— you're making too much noise, giving yourself away—

She went back across the corridor and ducked into a tiny alcove in front of one of the stores. She had to calm down, clear her mind—she had to *think!* Slowly her eyes searched the stores, the corners and hidden niches, the doorways, the plants and pools and benches and staircases. *He could be anywhere—anywhere!*

She moved out into the very center of the mall, turning in helpless circles, her hands to her head, trying not to scream, trying not to go crazy from sheer terror.

Again she started running, clumsily, painfully, her eyes darting back and forth—behind her—

I know you're here somewhere—where are you?

And then suddenly she stopped.

She was sure she'd felt something just then—a cold draft across her legs, a faint whiff of fresh air, a breeze blowing in from outside.

She was in another corridor now, with stores on either side, darkened window displays full of mannequins and shadows—and as she spotted the exit doors at the end of the hall, she stared in dismay.

One of them was standing wide open.

A gust of wind blew in, swirling dead leaves across the floor.

Trish gazed at the doorway for a long, long time. She could feel the skin prickling at the back of her neck—the gooseflesh rising along her arms. It had to be a trick. She knew he would never let her get away so easily. He was close now . . . very, very close . . . waiting to see what she would do. He was playing with her again . . . taking his time . . . and she let her eyes go slowly over the storefronts, over the windows, trying to find his hiding place.

Cautiously she started forward once more.

And as her eyes focused downward, she saw something in the open doorway and stared at it stupidly, her mind refusing to function, wondering who could have left it there and why.

It was a shopping bag.

It was just sitting there, all by itself, and she leaned over to look inside.

And she covered her mouth with her hands to keep from screaming—

Nita's sweater.

"No . . . no. . . ."

Trish whirled around and made for the nearest staircase. Her sobs burned in her throat, and her chest felt like it was on fire. As she moved along the upper corridor and saw The Latest Trend up ahead, she also saw the entrance, standing open, and the interior of the shop beyond, bathed in deep shadow.

"Nita!" she shrieked. "Nita—where *are* you?"

She thought she heard something.

A cry? a whimper?

It *sounded* like it was coming from the dressing rooms.

It sounded like it had called her name.

"Nita?" she murmured.

She took a cautious step forward. Almost unthinkingly, she reached out toward one of the display counters and picked up two of the heavy paperweights, clenching them tightly in her fists. Her eyes glanced nervously around at the counters and shelves and racks, but everything was deathly still.

She paused at the entrance to the dressing rooms and took a long careful look down the hallway. The curtains were tied back, and she could see into each of the tiny stalls.

Empty.

But I'm sure I heard something—I'm sure I did.

More than anything, she wanted to turn back, wanted to leave. *But what if it was Nita I heard—what if she's hurt and calling for help?*

But of course that was silly, Trish scolded herself. She could see every inch of the dressing area, and it was obvious that nobody was in it.

She took a few more steps—it was so cold in there. And it all came back to her again, that eerie feeling she'd had that day when she'd tried on the white dress, the draft she'd felt across her legs, the horrible, creeping suspicion that she wasn't alone.

And she was heading toward that same dressing room now, the one in the corner that wasn't entirely visible from the doorway, the one tucked back into the corner on the left side of the full-length mirror.

And as she got up to it, she stood and stared, her heart sinking into her stomach, her lips moving but no sound coming out.

Part of the dressing room wall was gone.

It was a small section located at the very back—an inconspicuous section near the floor—and it was completely missing, as though someone had simply come in and conveniently lifted out the panel.

And someone *was* here now—she was sure of it—someone behind her—moving softly—coming closer—

And as she whirled around in terror, he filled the

narrow doorway that led into the main part of the store, and he took a step toward her.

"Don't be afraid," the voice said softly, and she *knew* that voice—she'd heard that voice *before*—

"Don't be afraid of me," it said again, and he was coming closer now—*closer*—and she was backing away, trying to reach the door as his face moved into the shadows and she saw him reach slowly out to her.

"Trish," Wyatt whispered, "come with me."

"No!"

Trish threw the paperweights as hard as she could. She heard a sickening thud and a moan, and saw Wyatt stumble once, then drop to his knees. As she started past him, his hand shot out and grabbed her ankle, but she screamed and managed to shake him off, even as he struggled to get up off the floor.

In one split instant of despair, Trish realized that she was trapped.

She didn't hesitate now.

Turning back down the aisle, she ducked into the last dressing room and climbed through the hole in the wall.

For just a moment she thought she heard a soft yell behind her.

And as she looked back fearfully at the opening, she was just in time to see the panel slam back into place.

21

She was in total darkness.

For one split second, Trish froze, her mind unable to accept what was happening. And then she was throwing herself at the wall, pounding, screaming at the top of her lungs. The wall seemed solid beneath her fists; she couldn't hear any sort of movement from the other side.

Get hold of yourself! You can't panic—you have to keep a clear head.

Biting her lip, she pressed back against the wall and drew several long, deep breaths. She was shaking all over, and she felt icy cold. She didn't know whether to feel relatively safe now or more afraid than before. Wyatt obviously couldn't get to her in here—but where had he gone?

She banged again on the wall—banged and called until her hands ached and her throat hurt. No one was going to let her out of here. She had no choice but to go on. *But where?*

There seemed to be a little light now. As Trish squinted against the gloom, a fine filtery haze seemed to hang in the close, cramped air. Cautiously she moved forward, holding her hands out in front of her. It was impossible to stand up in here. She tried squatting on her heels and moving forward that way, but it was too uncomfortable. Finally she resorted to her hands and knees and began to crawl.

The passage turned almost at once—so sharply that she bumped into the wall. As she followed it around a corner, it suddenly grew in height so that she was able to stand again. It was only temporary relief—a niche no bigger than a closet—and as she paused to examine it, she was suddenly amazed to see a window reaching nearly from floor to ceiling. She peered at it closely and felt her breath catch in her throat.

She could see the hallway of the dressing area—the fitting rooms on either side.

I'm behind the mirror! This is a two-way mirror!

Instantly her cheeks flamed, remembering her eerie feeling of being watched that day. So that's what he'd meant about seeing her in and out of the white dress—he'd been watching her the whole time! She couldn't stand to think about it. She turned her head and went on.

Again the passageway shrank so that she was forced to her knees once more. She had no sense of distance or time in this dark place—she only knew that she had to go on, that she didn't have a choice. She didn't want to think about where it led or if, indeed, it led anywhere at all. The prospect of being walled up in here alive was more than she could bear.

Determinedly she forced the grim images from her

mind and kept going. Without warning, the passage stopped, and she hit the wall again, shocked.

She reached out and ran her hands across the splintery wood. She thought she could feel a tiny hole near the middle, and she worked her finger inside and pulled. Almost immediately a door popped open, and she thrust her arm across the threshold, terrified that there would be nothing beyond but air.

A stairway.

Trembling with relief, Trish worked her body sideways until she could feel the steps beneath her feet. The ceiling was a little higher here, and she started down, careful to keep her head low. The stairs seemed to go down and down forever. Once she stopped to catch her breath, but the horrible thoughts tried to crowd back into her mind, so she pushed them away and kept going.

This has to go somewhere . . . please, somewhere. . . .

She'd never gone down so many steps before. Her legs were aching, threatening to give out on her. She stopped, then stopped again, to rub her cramped muscles, then forced herself to keep going. It couldn't go on forever—or could it?

Finally, as her foot swung down toward another step, it hit level ground. Caught offguard, Trish stumbled and caught herself against the wall. Another dead end. Again she explored the wooden surface with her hands—again she discovered a knothole that turned out to be a door handle. Holding her breath, she tugged the door open.

A tunnel. As Trish stood and stared, she saw a dimly lit tunnel winding off ahead of her, and hazy darkness beyond. Steeling herself, she began to follow it, cringing away from the thick clots of spiderwebs that swung down from the low ceiling. The floor seemed to be made of packed earth, and it was slick in places where water had seeped through. She could see thick patches of slime on the stone walls.

She wondered how long she'd been following this maze—how long it had been since she'd left the mall to hunt for Imogene. *When will someone miss me? I wonder where Nita and Imogene are?* She wanted to cry, but she didn't. She wanted to scream and run and shriek with terror—but she made herself keep going because she knew she didn't have any other choice. And when it seemed that she'd been walking miles upon endless miles, and she finally spotted the door at the end of the tunnel, strangely enough, she felt nothing—nothing at all—only viewed it as another cruel joke that would lead her absolutely nowhere.

It was a massive door—heavy and of solid wood—and she didn't have to search for a way to open it. The huge iron bolt slid quite easily in her hand, and as Trish took hold of the latch, the door swung outward with a slow, rusty groan.

To her surprise she came face to face with another door.

There was no bolt on this one—just a tiny window carved into the top half, lined with metal bars.

Pausing a moment, she glanced behind her, and for one quick second she suddenly wanted to turn around and run—run back the way she'd come—run fast and far, far away from whatever was waiting on the other side of the door.

Slowly she stood on tiptoe, her fingers curling around the bars on the window.

There was a brief glimpse of darkness—shadows pulsing up stone walls—yet before she could make out anything else, she felt the door move beneath her weight.

Jumping back, she watched fearfully as the door opened inward, as the room beyond slipped into shadowy view. And as her eyes slowly began to adjust to the gloom, her lips parted in a soundless cry, and she reached out to steady herself against the threshold.

At first it seemed the room was full of clouds.

They were hanging everywhere—from the low stone ceiling—on the slick stone walls—swagged from corner to corner—layer upon layer of filmy whiteness swaying slightly from the breath of some damp, invisible breeze. As Trish stared at them, she suddenly noticed dark blotches scuttling from one gauzy drapery to another—and she realized with a shudder that they were actually cobwebs, infested with huge spiders.

She drew back to rub the goose bumps from her arms, and as she did so, one of the spiders dropped from overhead onto her shoulder. Screaming, Trish hit it onto the floor and tried to jump away, immediately entangling herself in more of the sticky webs. Gasping for air, she fought to peel the sticky threads from her face, her neck, her hair, but the more she struggled, the more they wound around her, like wrappings around a mummy. To her horror she felt spiders running across her scalp, the scurry of tiny legs along her cheeks, down her throat—and she screamed and screamed, at last twisting herself free and falling onto the damp floor.

Sobbing, she reached out a hand to push herself up. . . .

And felt her fingers close around someone's foot.

Trish screamed again and scrambled backward, her eyes lifting in terror to the figure towering above.

And as her eyes focused on the face—the head with no hair—the painted eyes—the arm held stiffly aloft —she froze upon her knees and wondered if she was truly losing her mind.

A mannequin.

It was a mannequin standing there, staring off into nothingness.

And yet—it wasn't alone.

As Trish turned her head, a slow, cold numbness crept over her. The room was *full* of mannequins— some male, some female, in various stages of dress and undress, some without limbs, without hair, some without heads. Some clustered in groups, as if they'd been interrupted from some private conversation at her intrusion, while others stood all by themselves and watched their comrades—the walls—her.

Swallowing hard, Trish sat back on her heels, her brain trying to function, to take it all in.

She could see the sconces now, burning and sputtering from their niches in the stones. The room was throbbing with shadows. The frozen faces of the mannequins flickered in and out of light, and the walls seemed to pulse with a life of their own. As Trish's eyes went dazedly over the lifesize dolls . . . the cobwebs . . . the shadows . . . she saw that the room went even further back—way beyond where any reflection could reach. Slowly she got up and walked to the edge of the light.

It was as if certain rooms were defined by specific shadows, and where this room ended, another began in a different sort of light—calmer and dimmer. Trish could see candles burning atop a long wooden table . . . the sturdy wooden chairs placed around. To her amazement, she saw plates and platters of food arranged there . . . goblets of wine . . . a three-tiered wedding cake. . . .

"Oh, no . . . no. . . ."

She moved back farther into the chamber and saw a wooden cupboard . . . a washstand with a basin and old-fashioned pitcher. A handcarved cradle. A huge wooden bed with white canopy and snowy bed-curtains. . . .

Mesmerized, she turned and looked back, held for a moment by a roomful of lifeless stares. She moved forward slowly, her hand extended, touching the table, the chairs—seeing but not believing, here yet strangely not here.

And then she saw it . . . draped carefully over the covers of the bed. . . .

The white dress.

The white dress she'd put on in front of the mirror.

Gasping, she whirled around, but she was too late.

A tall dark figure blocked her path, and the candles guttered wildly and threatened to go out.

"Trish," he whispered lovingly, "I knew you'd come."

22

What have you done with Nita and Imogene?" she asked.

And it was funny, she thought from somewhere deep, deep in her consciousness. Now that she was finally here, now that the inevitable had finally happened, it was more like a dream than real—as if some other power within her was keeping her on her feet, making her talk, holding her together.

"My friends," she said, and she tried to keep her voice from shaking, but she knew he could hear it—knew he could see her trembling. "What have you *done* with them?"

"Ah, yes. Nita and Imogene."

He was still hidden in the shadows where she couldn't see his face, and the flickering light made him seem immensely large, yet insubstantial—like a dark ghost from a dark fantasy. Trish felt herself move away from him until her back rested against the table.

"I found Nita's sweater by the door," Trish choked out. "And that phone call *wasn't* from Imogene, was it—it was you."

"And you passed both tests beautifully," he said softly. "Just as I knew you would."

"What—what do you mean?"

"Freedom for yourself—or help for your friends." He sighed, as if slightly in awe of her decision. "No matter. Both of them are quite safe. As a matter of fact, they're probably home right now with no earthly idea what a sacrifice you made on their behalf."

"But—but Nita's sweater. And Imogene was gone—"

"Yes, gone on a wild-goose chase, but she *did* come back." He seemed to be thinking. "And Nita's sweater —she bought a new one, you see, and wore it home. That's all. That's all it was."

"But—"

"You can believe me, Trish—I saw her trying it on myself. She stood in front of the mirror, and she looked just lovely in it. But not as lovely as you. And then she simply left the old sweater at the store by mistake. I'll make sure she finds it when she comes back to work."

Trish's knees felt weak. She sagged backward, then stiffened again as she saw him move.

"But let's not talk about Nita and Imogene," he murmured. "Let's talk about you. About us."

"Wyatt," she begged, "please—" And the whole time he was talking to her, she kept thinking how different his voice sounded when he was whispering like that—so different from the way he talked when he was bussing tables—when they'd eaten at the deli that night. And not just his voice, but everything— everything about him so different.

"Wyatt," she said again, but he began to laugh—a slow, deep laugh that sent shivers up her spine.

"No, Trish, guess again. And don't confuse me with someone who has such little class. It . . . offends me."

He seemed to shift his position, and for one panicky moment Trish couldn't distinguish him from the shadows. *What have I done—what did I do to Wyatt— what was he doing in the store?* She began inching sideways along the table, trying to put distance between them. She heard him chuckle again.

"It won't do you any good—you can't run away from me here. And why would you? I know how to make you happy, Trish. I know what you like. What you *need* . . ."

"Please." She looked frantically around for an escape, but tried to keep her face expressionless. "Why are you doing this? Why won't you tell me who you are?"

"But I did tell you. My name is Athan. And I'm doing this . . . because I love you."

"But you can't—not really," she said quickly. "You can't possibly feel that way about me—you don't even know me."

"But I *do* know you. I've watched you for a long, long time. While you work . . . with your friends . . . in the parking lot . . . in the library . . ."

"No," she whispered, "don't—"

"I've watched you go to school . . . and go home. I've watched you in the hospital . . . and in the mirror . . ."

"Stop!" Trish cried. *"Please* let me go! *Please!"*

"And that night in the woods—at that cabin—your face in the moonlight—"

"Stop it!"

"From the first moment I ever saw you, I knew you were the one I'd been waiting for—the one I wanted to share my world with."

He stepped forward, his silhouette hovering at the very edge of the darkness. She could see his arms lift, as if embracing all the shadows in the room.

"*This* is my world, Trish. I've created it with my own hands. No one is allowed here without my consent. No one is allowed to come . . . and no one is allowed to leave."

He turned abruptly, walking away from her, weaving in and out slowly between the mannequins.

"Whatever I've needed, I've simply taken from above. From stores. From delivery trucks." He sounded amused. "Even from careless shoppers. There's no trick to it, really. This whole mall *belongs* to me. No one knows it like I do. I've lived here such a long, long time, I know every inch of it—above *and* below. I *let* them come, you know—I don't like intruders, but I *let* them come above. To walk. To stare. To spend their silly money. But down *here*"—his tone sounded dreamy—"down here, it's *my* domain. Down here . . . I am *king.*"

For a moment Trish thought he'd forgotten her. She glanced around wildly, but the only escape seemed to be through the door she'd come in by. He paused, as if thinking, then started back toward her again.

"My world has been a world nearly complete unto itself, do you see?" Again he gestured, his hands ghostly shadows against shadows. "The only thing missing was . . . you."

Trish felt her body go cold. She had reached the edge of the table and now she eased around to the other side.

"I've waited for you my whole life," he murmured softly. "Your beauty . . . your sweetness . . ." He drew a long, shaky breath. "Your love."

"No . . ." Trish whispered.

"No one could love you as I do. And now I can show you how much. Now we have forever . . . for me to show you just how much I can love you."

She was backing away now—farther into the chamber—beside the cupboard—beside the bed—

She never actually saw him coming. He moved with such speed—such silent grace—that his arms were around her before she even realized what was happening.

"No!" she screamed. "Let me go! You killed Bethany, didn't you? You *murdered* her!"

"I did it for *you!*" He wrestled her arms down to her sides, pinning her with frightening strength. She struggled only an instant, then went quiet in his grasp, her heart pounding out of control. *Go along with him— don't make him mad—don't make him hurt you.*

"I did it for you," he said, and he sounded angry now, his words coming between clenched teeth. "She made you unhappy. She humiliated you, she *hurt* you! And I won't stand for *anyone* hurting you."

His head was still pulled back into the shadows. As Trish peered up at him, her mind raced feverishly, stalling for time.

"I—I know," she stammered, trying so hard to get the words out, to sound sincere. "I—I know you did it for me. I know—I know you care about me—"

"More than anyone. More than anything."

"And I know you want me all to yourself—that you only want me to be happy."

He was nodding—she could feel his body giving a little, his grip on her arms relaxing.

"So why won't you let me see you?" she coaxed. "Now that I'm here—why don't you let me see your face?"

He was silent for so long that she was afraid she'd made him angry. She pulled back a little, but he grabbed her tighter, pressing her up against his chest.

"You've seen me before. Many times."

"What—what are you—"

He released her so roughly that she stumbled backward, sprawling across the bed. Terrified, she saw him towering over her, his tall form bending over . . . lower . . . lower. . . .

She saw his hand reach out toward the table beside her . . . saw the quick spurt of a match . . . saw the glow of a lamp as it trickled golden light across his face. . . .

She saw the thick, curly hair . . . the scar . . . the dark glasses. . . .

She saw him put one hand to his head.

Pull off the wig.

Drop the glasses onto the coverlet.

Peel the scar slowly from his cheek.

"My God," Trish whispered.

"You've seen me in store windows . . . posing with my mannequin friends. And in The Eatery reading my newspaper. You've seen me in work clothes and delivery clothes—as a mailman, as a salesman, doing repair work and maintenance and emptying trash. I've been a security guard and an usher in the theaters —I've shopped and pushed brooms and handed out flyers. I've got a million disguises—and I never have to look the same way twice."

"You killed that other girl, too, didn't you?" Trish was scooting back across the covers now, trying to get away from him, from the horrible smug smile on his face. "You were taking her body out to the trash when I came in that night."

"That was unfortunate," he sighed, his expression annoyed. "Freida got too curious. She found that secret panel in The Latest Trend—I had no choice. She would have told someone—they would have started looking *around* down here. I couldn't have intruders ruining our lives!"

She was shaking her head, still edging away from him, trying to get to the other side of the bed.

"I could have taken you that night," he mused, thinking back, shaking his head slowly. "In fact, I almost did. But don't you see—I wasn't quite ready yet. And you were . . . distraught. And I wanted everything to be perfect. Perfect for *you*. The wedding feast"—he waved his hand toward the table, toward the elegant array of food—"the wedding dress"—he reached out and ran one hand slowly down her arm . . . her hip . . . over the smooth white counterpane—"the wedding bed."

"No," Trish whispered. "Please."

"Put this on," he said, and he snatched the dress roughly from the bed, throwing it into her lap. "Tonight is our marriage ceremony. I want you in this."

And she was crying now, tears streaming down her cheeks, and impulsively she reached out to him, pleading—

"Roger—Roger—don't—"

But he grabbed her and shook her, and his green eyes were wild with rage.

"I'm *not Roger!*" he shouted. "I'm *Athan!*" His voice shook, faltered. He pushed her away and turned toward the wall. "You know what it means, don't you?" he mumbled, yet he sounded as though he were talking to himself—as if he'd suddenly forgotten she was even there. "You know what Athan means."

Trish could hardly speak, she was so scared. "I—I don't—"

"Immortality," he whispered.

He looked back over his shoulder. His eyes narrowed . . . a dark smile played over his lips.

"Immortality," he said again. "My wedding gift to you."

23

There." He pointed, and as Trish followed the direction of his arm, she saw a screen hidden in a dark corner. "You can change over there."

She felt dizzy and strangely faint. She could see his shadow pulsing up the wall. She could still hear him speaking, yet he sounded miles away.

"I'm the one who got you—*I* am! I saw you talking to *him*—but *I'm* the one you were saved for! He's been *following* me. He thinks he's so clever, but he's no match! He's been following me so he could take you *away* from me—but I've *finished* with him once and for all!"

His voice was getting higher—breathless and agitated. As Trish listened numbly, he began pacing back and forth along the wall, rubbing his hands together.

"Following me—*both* of them! But *he's* the one who wanted you—*he's* the one who put his hands on

you—who touched you—and—and kissed you—"
He broke off abruptly, his body quivering with deep,
ragged breaths. "He will *never* touch you again! He
will *never* be forgiven—*I'm* the only god in this
world!"

Trish heard her own voice, scarcely a whisper.
"Who . . . who are you talking about?" she murmured, and yet deep down she knew, with a cold sick
feeling inside, she knew, and her heart broke and
shattered.

"You should have known better!" Athan turned on
her. "You tried to play with my feelings, but you
should have realized all along that *I'd* be the one to
win!" He paced several feet, then back again, and a
deep laugh bubbled low in his throat. "I left *him* by
the loading docks—with an ice pick in his heart."

And instantly an image came back to her—an
image so horrible that her hand flew to her throat to
hold back a scream. *Going through that winding
tunnel to find Imogene—that presence on the other
side of that wall—the bloody hand holding the ice
pick. . . .* And she'd run away because she'd thought it
was *Athan*—she'd thought it was a *murderer. Only it
wasn't Athan—it wasn't Roger at all. It was Storm—it
must have been Storm!*

"No—" Her voice trembled, but Athan rushed on.

"I told you not to talk to anyone. I told you not to
tell *anyone.*"

"I didn't—you've got to believe—"

"You *talked* to him! You let him hold you! When
you were already meant only for me!"

"No—no—it's not like that at all—"

"It's something I can't allow," he said with sudden
calm. "You understand, of course. It's something I
can—*never*—allow."

The room swayed around her. Her palm went to her forehead, and she grabbed out for the wall.

"He has no place here. No place in our world. Threats like that must be destroyed, so I did the only thing I could do." He paused a moment as if thinking. "As for the other one"—again that slow satisfied smile in his voice—"you finally—*finally*—realized that you and I were destined. I knew you would. And when you hurt that other one, when you turned on him and hurt him so that we—you and I—could be together, it made me so . . . completely . . . happy. Merciful, really. But that's so like you, Trish. Merciful and kind and perfect. He'll never feel a thing when I go back to finish the job."

"What—what are you talking about—"

"Please. Your wedding dress," he said softly, and his shadow flickered wildly as he approached her. "I want to see you in it. Let's have no more talk about . . . unpleasant things."

His hand moved to her neck . . . trailed down across her shoulders. She lowered her head and tried hard not to cringe.

"I respect your shyness," he said softly, giving a deep bow. "And I even find it quite charming. Things will be different. When you've had time to get to know me."

For several moments he stood there, his brows drawn together thoughtfully. Then he leaned across the bed and pinned her with his eyes.

"But right now I must attend to this . . . business. I trust you'll be . . . less shy . . . when I come back again."

Somehow she managed to nod. As his eyes raked over her body, she gave an imperceptible shiver and forced herself to look back at him. And then he was going out the door, and she heard the horrible grating of metal and realized that he had locked her in.

Her head fell forward, and hysterical sobs rose in her throat. She choked them back down and flattened herself against the wall, her eyes frantically sweeping the chamber, the ceiling—even the floor. *I've got to get out of here—I can't be here when he gets back—*

Storm's face—the strength of him, the warmth of him as he'd pressed her close. Trish covered her face with her hands and gave in to total despair. *Why didn't I trust him? Where is he? If he dies, it's all my fault.*

And Wyatt. Is that where Roger's going now—to finish him off?

I have to think—I have to think of something.

She stumbled to her feet, putting out her hands, feeling her way around the bed. Her head was so light, she could hardly stand up—she could hardly see where she was going. The room flickered around her—confusing her, tricking her. She could feel the mannequins watching her—their painted eyes *following* her as she tried to walk. *Help me! Help me, somebody!* Spiderwebs floated out to her, plastering themselves to her face, molding themselves over her mouth so she couldn't scream.

It seemed to take hours to get to the door. She wrapped her hands around the latch and pulled and pulled. She could feel her strength giving out—the handle was the only thing holding her up. *Maybe he didn't really go away. Maybe he's really hiding just on the other side, waiting to see what I'll do, and when he hears me trying to escape, he'll be so furious.*

The thought sobered her at once and she sagged against the door, gasping for breath. She beat weakly against the heavy wood, then looked wildly around for a weapon—something—*anything!* How long would it take before he came back again? And what frame of mind would he be in? She felt his hands again on her shoulders, and she shuddered violently and felt sick. *I'll die before I let him touch me—I'll kill myself.*

The table.

With a surge of hope, she went back to the dinner table, fumbling through the table settings, searching for a knife. There wasn't one. Frantically she searched everywhere—no carving knife, no corkscrew—not even a fork. *Damn him!* She dropped into a chair and eyed the wedding feast with pure contempt. Apparently, he'd thought of everything—even her desperate measures to get away.

A wine goblet.

Hurriedly, she curled her fingers around one of the crystal stems. She gritted her teeth and prepared to hit the glass against the edge of the table.

And then she heard someone at the door.

Trish's heart leaped into her throat and she jumped up, cowering behind the table, the goblet forgotten, her eyes wide and focused on the other side of the room.

She saw the latch quiver slightly . . . as if from the touch of a stealthy hand.

The door began to move. It hesitated—then came open with an eerie groan.

"Trish!" came the urgent whisper. "Trish—are you in here?"

And she was inching out from behind the table, drifting between the cobwebs, terrified—hopeful—as the shadow moved cautiously out of the darkness and came toward her.

"Trish? God, look at this place! Are you okay?"

And she could see his face now, in the half light, a

shiny trail of blood down one cheek, and the gun, pointed upward, at his shoulder.

"Wyatt," she mumbled, "is that you?"

"Come on—hurry."

She was almost to him when the door suddenly creaked and something scraped outside.

"Put out the lights!" he hissed, and as she hesitated, she saw the gun move, waving her into action. "The lights! Do it!"

He was a blur—rushing along the walls, flinging down the sconces, stomping them with his boots—and she began to run, too, blowing out the lamp beside the bed, dousing the candles on the table. The room grew fainter around her—mannequins fading one by one into nothingness—and as her terrified eyes sought the last spark of light and saw it die, the room plunged into a sudden blackness worse than any night.

Trish couldn't see her hand in front of her face.

Frozen in an endless, empty void, she was terrified to move—to reach out—to breathe.

"Where—" she began, but the door groaned slowly on its hinges . . . echoing on . . . and on . . . and on. . . .

She felt the dank, cold draft swirling the spiderwebs around her head. . . .

And she knew that Athan had come back for her.

24

Trish expected any second to be snatched from the darkness.

What she didn't expect was the sudden thud of bodies colliding and rolling over the floor—the groans—the shouts—a sharp outcry of pain.

"Police!" Wyatt shouted. "Freeze, dammit! *Police!*"

Without any warning a gun went off—explosions echoing back and back and back through endless caverns of night. Trish screamed and covered her ears.

"I'm a cop!" Wyatt yelled again. "Freeze!"

"Let go!" a second voice answered back. "It's me, you idiot!"

The scuffling stopped. As Trish huddled in her pocket of darkness, she heard a moan and then Wyatt's voice, tense and angry.

"Where the *hell* have you been, anyway?"

"Was that my gun or yours?" the other voice groaned.

198

"I . . . think it was mine. Are you okay?"

"Are you?"

"No . . . I think I just shot myself."

"*Shot* yourself?"

"Relax. It's just a scratch."

"Way to go, Wyatt."

And Trish recognized that other voice, weak and breathless as it was—

"Come on," Storm mumbled, "we've got to get out of here."

"Well, Christ, you're bleeding all *over* the place—"

"Are you sure that's not you? Where's Trish?"

At last something stirred within her, allowing her to move. She called out, her voice trembling, in terror and in relief.

"I'm here—I'm all right."

She heard Wyatt curse under his breath and then there was a slow, sliding sound, as if one of them had dragged the other to his feet.

"Come on," Wyatt hissed. "Trish—come on—"

"I can't see you," she called back fearfully. "I can't see a thing."

"You got a light?" Wyatt mumbled. There was a moment of silence, and then he swore again. "Follow my voice, Trish. Just keep following my voice."

Yet even as Trish took a cautious step, her heart was suddenly gripped with wild, uncontrollable terror, and she froze again in her tracks. The blackness sucked her in, holding her, pinning her. And the breeze was cold, cold across the floor, stirring old forgotten smells of mildew and rot—and something else, *something.* . . .

"I can't," she whispered back, and she could feel her spine tingling with absolute terror. . . . Danger—*danger!* And the hair lifted at the back of her neck, and her heart fluttered like a dying bird, caught in her throat—

"Trish—"

"I can't!" she screamed.

"You have to!" Wyatt shouted back. "Trish—come *on!*"

She forced herself forward, plunging through the darkness, sweeping the emptiness with her hands, the spiderwebs gagging her, the uneven floor slippery beneath her feet.

"You're doing fine," Storm gasped. "Keep coming —we're right here—right—"

And suddenly she *knew* why she was so terrified. Because that horrible deathly feeling *hadn't* gone away—not even when she'd heard Storm's voice, when she'd actually thought for a moment, wanted to believe, that it was *only* Storm who'd slipped into the room on a breath of stale, decaying air—

"He's here," she whispered, and her voice rose, panic-stricken. "Can't you feel it? He's *here!*"

And the mannequins were all around her now— hollow bodies closing in—arms reaching—fingers clawing. Her frenzied hands slid over mocking smiles, staring eyes, stiff human corpses touching her, holding her—

"Don't move," Wyatt ordered calmly. "Stay right where you are, Trish—don't make any noise."

She froze. The pounding of her heart was like a drum in her head. Fear coursed behind her eyes in endless, rushing waves.

She knew she was going to faint. She took one faltering step and felt the mannequin pressing hard against her back.

She felt the rough, warm layers of clothing. . . .

The broad expanse of chest. . . .

She felt the mannequin breathe.

And as his arm came down around her neck, she felt her scream cut off before it even reached her lips.

"She's mine," Athan hissed. "And no one's going to take her from me."

"Let her go," Storm spoke up. His voice sounded even weaker now—he was struggling to breathe. "This is between us—you don't want her to get hurt."

"I'll kill her before I let you have her," Athan said calmly. "She *wants* to be with me. We need to be together."

"Then why don't you ask her!" Wyatt called. "Why don't you ask her who she'd rather be with?"

"She loves *me! I'm* the only one in her life—this is *our* world! You can't come in here—I won't let you spoil everything, do you hear me!"

Trish's heart nearly stopped as she felt an icy sting against her cheek. The metal point went slowly down the side of her face . . . down along her neck . . . her shoulder.

She could feel the ice pick poised right over her heart.

"*You* ask her!" Athan's voice was outraged, and his hold tightened around her throat. "*You* ask her how serious I am—she'll tell you how much I love her! She'll tell you what I'll do to make sure we stay together!"

"He's right!" Trish twisted her head, managed somehow to choke out the words. "He'll kill me. No matter what you do, it won't make any difference about me now. He means what he says."

"Let her go," Wyatt growled.

The tip of the ice pick punctured her blouse, and Trish whimpered.

"Never," Athan hissed. "Tonight is our wedding night. Tonight will go as planned."

Trish gagged as he squeezed on her neck. She heard a confused rush of sound near the doorway and a low chuckle from Athan's throat.

"Congratulate us," he whispered hoarsely. "We're going to say our vows."

His grip tightened again, and gasping for breath, Trish felt him pull her backward, dragging her across the floor. As she bumped and slid against him, she could feel her skirt twisting in the struggle—winding around her legs—and something scraping her, digging into her thigh as she fought to get free.

And as it hit her in that split second what she was going to do, she closed her eyes and prayed before she could lose her nerve.

"Wyatt!" she screamed.

As her free hand jerked the flashlight from her skirt and aimed the tiny pinprick of light upwards, she twisted sideways, straining against Athan's arm. She felt the last gasp of air cutting off from her windpipe, the fuzzy downward spiral as the blackness faded to nothing.

From somewhere far away the air shrieked with bullets.

And whatever was still managing to hold her up began at last to sag . . . to crumple . . . to fall . . . down . . . forever down. . . .

Taking her with it.

25

Something was on her mouth.

As Trish's eyes fluttered open, she felt something soft and insistent pressing against her lips, and as her eyes widened in confusion, she saw the darkness draw back, leaving a pair of steady brown eyes in its place.

"Yeah." Wyatt grinned. "You're okay."

"What—" Trish tried to sit up, and Wyatt slid an arm beneath her shoulders, propping her against him.

"Mouth to mouth," Storm groaned. "You're supposed to be *reviving* her—that's *all* you're supposed to be doing."

"She's fine. Which is more than I can say for you." Wyatt glanced down at his arm and grimaced. "Or actually . . . for me."

Storm groaned again, and as Trish's eyes slowly adjusted to the light, she looked wildly around the gloomy interior of Athan's room. Off to her right an indistinct shape lay prone on the floor. Instantly she felt a hand slide firmly under her chin and force her head around.

"He's dead," Wyatt said matter-of-factly. "You don't want to see."

"But—but—how—"

"If it hadn't been for that flashlight," Storm mumbled weakly. "If it hadn't been for your quick thinking—"

"Quick thinking!" Wyatt snorted. "What about my quick *shooting!*"

"Yeah. About as quick as a slug." Storm sighed. "How many times did you *have* to shoot before you finally *hit* him?"

"So I didn't get him on the first try. Big deal." Wyatt shrugged and patted Trish on the shoulder. "You okay?"

"I think so. Storm . . ."

She crawled over to where he was lying, where Wyatt had propped him up against the wall and covered him with blankets. There was blood on the floor, and his face was ghostly pale.

"Oh, Storm—"

"It's okay." He managed a feeble smile. "It's probably not as bad as it looks."

"I don't understand—none of this is making sense."

"We've had our eye on ol' Roger here for a long time." Wyatt sighed, positioning himself next to Storm, leaning back against the wall. "Things around the mall disappearing—*people* around the mall disappearing—except we just never could quite figure out how he was doing it."

"And you two are policemen?" Trish stared at both of them in amazement.

"Undercover." Storm nodded, looking a little

ashamed of the ruse. "And we've had our eyes on *you* for a long time, too."

"Sorry to disappoint you," Wyatt added, "but you're not the first love-of-his-life Roger's fixated on. Other girls have disappeared through the years—only nobody ever found them. Only thing they seemed to have in common was that they came here to shop—or work—or both."

"Kidnapping them," Storm began.

"Killing them," Wyatt clarified.

"Whatever," Storm finished, "seems to satisfy him for a while. Months. Seasons. But it doesn't last. And then he has to find someone else."

"The mall wanted to keep it quiet." Wyatt looked down at his gun and laid it to the side. "Bad publicity. Plus the fact that no one could ever prove a damn thing."

"How old are you anyway?" Trish was still staring at Storm, who managed a weak smile.

"Older than I look," he said.

"*Much* older than he looks," Wyatt said.

"We've got to get him out of here." Trish turned anxiously to Wyatt. "He's lost so much blood."

"Well, excuse me—I'll just give him a pint or two of mine," Wyatt said dryly. He shifted uncomfortably and Trish saw the blood-soaked rag tied around his arm.

"Oh, Wyatt—I'm so sorry—"

"Help's on the way." Wyatt waved a hand at her. "Hey, I radioed on my way down. Don't worry."

"We suspected he'd targeted you or one of your friends," Storm went on, as Trish moved closer to him. "We'd started noticing him—or, should I say, one of the characters he played—in The Eatery, and then Nita's store got hit.

"And that girl disappeared," Wyatt broke in.

"So we watched you three. Followed you. Even checked out your cars after you got here and before you went home."

"You *were* breaking into my car that night!" she turned to Wyatt accusingly.

"I broke into your car lots of times." He sounded bored.

"But he didn't find that tape until after you got to work this morning." Storm shifted, gritting his teeth. "Or now is it yesterday morning? What time is it, anyway?"

Wyatt looked down at his wrist and shrugged. "Forgot my watch. Oh, well."

"Then how did you finally know it was me he was after?" Trish wanted to know.

"We were watching you the night you went out to check your car," Storm said, almost guiltily. "So we saw when you got that call in the parking lot. Except —then—we weren't exactly sure what was going on—how Roger was going to play it this time."

"Yeah." Wyatt nodded. "We knew you were pretty upset about something. We figured he was getting lonely again."

"And then you had that accident on the escalator," Storm went on. "I kept trying to get you to admit to me that you'd been running from something. I kept thinking if you'd just confide in me, we'd be able to do something!"

"But you were a jerk about it," Wyatt sighed. "You wouldn't say a word."

"I couldn't!" Trish protested. "He said he'd hurt my friends!"

"I *told* you that's what the reason probably was."

Wyatt glanced over at Storm. "Didn't I tell you that's what the reason probably was?"

"And then that night at the cabin, I was *still* trying to get you to open up to me—" Storm began, but Wyatt started laughing.

"And that was the absolutely stupidest story I ever heard in my life! That whole thing about the crazy lady—where the hell did you come up with that!"

Trish looked from one to the other, her mind spinning.

"Wait a minute. So you followed us there?"

"Sure," Wyatt said.

"And that's why you were outside Nita's house that night?"

"Great detective," Storm mumbled. "So good at being inconspicuous."

"Well, I found that tape this morning, didn't I?" Wyatt defended himself.

"Yeah, finally. Not that you had to unravel any great clues—the stupid thing was *lying* right there in her front seat."

"Don't talk," Trish ordered him. Then, after thinking a moment, she added, "So you *knew* something was going to happen tonight?"

They both nodded, and she looked at them in dismay.

"We were trying to watch all of you—you and Nita and Imogene. So when I saw Imogene running off to the loading docks, I followed her," Storm admitted.

"And I saw *her* come back again, but not you." Wyatt frowned at Storm.

"Yeah, well, thanks a lot for coming to rescue me," Storm muttered. "Hell, I didn't even hear the guy coming—he slipped up behind me in the hall and yanked me back into a utility closet and—" He winced, gently fingering his ribcage. "If someone hadn't been coming down the tunnel when they did, I wouldn't have had a chance. I guess it distracted him. It threw off his aim. He got out of there pretty fast. And the next thing I knew, *you* were down there."

"I didn't know that was you," Trish said miserably. "I was coming around the curve in the tunnel, and I thought you were the murderer—"

"While I was trying to warn you," Storm broke in. "Not so easy, since I could hardly even stand up."

"I just got so scared, I ran off and left you there."

"I know." Storm nodded, then managed a smile, as if the whole thing amused him. "Thanks a lot."

"Don't talk," Trish put a hand over his mouth, smiling back. "You need to save your strength."

Wyatt picked up the story. "And in the meantime, I couldn't find anybody anywhere. Until I saw Trish in the mall again. By that time everything was closed down, and I'd been looking in every hall and tunnel and stairway I could find."

"We knew about *some* of the tunnels," Storm added. "But not all of them. We never dreamed there were so many—this place is like a honeycomb with all that stuff underneath the mall."

"When I saw you, you were going into Nita's store," Wyatt told Trish. "So I ran upstairs to try and get you out."

"And I hit him with a paperweight," Trish admitted, much to Storm's amusement.

"You *are* a big help, aren't you?" he teased. "Well, it couldn't have hurt him much, if you got him in the head."

Wyatt grimaced and gingerly fingered the knot on

his scalp through his hair. "I don't think I was ever *completely* out—just dazed. I had these weird feelings of things going on, except I couldn't figure them out."

"Then you didn't hurt him," Storm said emphatically. "He's like that *normally.*"

Wyatt gave him a sarcastic look and continued the story. "Our friend here was in a big hurry to get you all to himself—so I think he was going to come back and finish me off afterward."

"But how did you know where I was?" Trish frowned. She tucked the blanket higher around Storm's shoulders, and Wyatt cleared his throat loudly.

"I saw him closing up the wall—putting that panel back in. So I pretended to be unconscious, and I waited till he'd left, and then I followed you. I figured wherever *you* ended up was where I'd find *him.*"

"So I was bait!" Trish burst out indignantly.

"Well . . ." Wyatt looked deadpan. "Sure. What'd you think?"

"Not bait," Storm sighed, giving Wyatt a reproachful look. "He was *trying* to protect you, in his own misguided way." He paused to take several deep breaths, then proceeded more cautiously. "We knew there had to be more than one route to wherever Roger was hiding, but he always just disappeared too fast or managed to lose us in the mall whenever we tried to tail him."

"So he must have known you were after him," she concluded. "He told me that *you* weren't what you seemed to be."

"Oh, he knew all right." Wyatt nodded. "And he also knew Storm was his number one rival."

Trish blushed as Wyatt grinned at her. "But I know"—she nodded wisely—"it was just another police tactic, right? Using me as bait again?"

"No," Storm said softly. "I don't think so." He reached for her hand and squeezed it. "Roger was pretty slippery. The only reason I found a way in tonight is because he came back to hide Bethany's body. After he took care of that gory little detail, I managed to follow him back here."

Trish shook her head, fighting the memory away. "He said . . . he said he did it for me."

"No," Storm said gently. "You can't ever think that *any* of this was your fault—in *any* way."

Wyatt raised one eyebrow, his voice solemnly matter-of-fact. "Hey. You would have been next."

"He's right," Storm echoed. "Roger knew you'd have to end up here once you got into the crawl-space—there was no other way out that you knew about."

"And just as he was leaving, I showed up," Wyatt broke in again. "So I decided—hey—maybe I should get you out."

"Nice of you," Storm murmured.

"Yeah," Wyatt nodded. "I thought so."

Storm's voice was fading, and Trish looked at Wyatt in alarm.

"We have to get him out of here. Listen to him—he's so weak."

"He'll be fine," Wyatt said, but he stood and looked down at Trish, regarding her quizzically. "The ambulance should be here by now, and I didn't want to move him around till I had to. I bandaged him good and tight and got the bleeding stopped, and now I'm going to carry him up to the mall. *With* my injured arm. Hey"—and a faint smile played at the corners of his mouth—"I'm not going to let him die on me. *Or you*. Okay?"

Trish stared at him a long moment. "Okay." She smiled back.

"So would you mind holding that flashlight again? So I don't fall and break my neck?"

"Or mine?" Storm reminded him weakly. "And could you put me in a comfortable spot? Preferably away from your shoulder blade?"

"Don't push your luck," Wyatt warned him.

Trish aimed the flashlight across the threshold and stood aside to hold the doors.

"And anyway, who's the hero around here?" Wyatt muttered, pulling Storm to his feet, hoisting Storm to his shoulder. "I mean, who shot the bad guy? Who saved the girl? Not that it seems to make any difference to anyone."

"I bet I know someone it would make a difference to," Trish couldn't help teasing. "Don't you know the more you intentionally ignore Nita, the more she's going to flirt with you?"

Wyatt looked back over his shoulder at her, the corners of his mouth lifting in a slow grin.

"Sure. I know that."

Trish stood aside as they went out. She could hear the sharp echo of Wyatt's boots against stone, and as she turned again toward the chamber, just for a moment she played the tiny beam of her flashlight back through the deep, deep shadows of the room.

She saw the wedding cake on the table.

And the long white dress in a heap upon the floor.

And where Roger's body lay so still, darkness had silently slipped in and taken over, so that he seemed to have completely disappeared.

Yet as Trish turned to go, an icy chill cut jaggedly through her veins and into the pit of her heart.

A trick of the light, that's all it is—shadows . . . cobwebs . . . fears. . . .

For just an instant, she'd let her flashlight play across the mannequins. . . .

And she could almost swear that one of them had moved.